"Cyndy's books are not only fun, they'r[e] ... recipes are nothing less than a waistline felon ... [Ho]se Bride

D0831655

"Laugh-out-loud humor and recipes to ... [de]lightful contemporary characters and a page-turning mystery that will make you want to pull out your bell-bottoms and tuck a flower behind your ear. Highly recommended."

ALLISON BOTTKE—Founder, God Allows U-Turns; Author, *A Stitch in Time*

"It's time to rejoin the ladies of the Friday Afternoon Club for more fun, friendship, and food. Once again Cyndy Salzmann has penned a tale that will make you long for a Friday Afternoon Club of your very own. Forget the laundry, find your stash of chocolates, and escape with the lovable members of the FAC. You'll be glad you did!"

JUDITH MILLER—Author, *In the Company of Secrets* and the Freedom's Path series

"Clever, thoughtful, humorous and more, Crime & Clutter *is one book you don't want to miss! My heart broke for the cost of poorly made choices and rejoiced for the redemptive power of forgiveness.*"

GAYLE ROPER—Author, *Caught in the Middle, Caught in the Act, Caught in a Bind,* and *Caught Redhanded*

"Good friends, good eats, and a juicy mystery, Crime & Clutter *kept me turning pages well into the night! A story of choices and heartache, of redemption and second chances . . . and great recipes to boot!*"

SUSAN MAY WARREN—Author, *Reclaiming Nick*

"Cyndy's ebullient personality colors her characters as she conveys family and friendship in all its joys and exasperations. Her book stirs together a collage of recipes, 1960s flashbacks, and contemporary scenes full of humor and insights."

SHARON HINCK—Author, *The Secret Life of Becky Miller* and *Renovating Becky Miller*

"Salzmann serves up a poignant mix of laughter and tears in this new Friday Afternoon Club Mystery. Crime & Clutter *takes readers on a gripping journey into the past as painful episodes from the turbulent 1960s shed light on a mystery in the present. Memorable characters and a satisfying twist at the end make for a must-read.*"

JILL ELIZABETH NELSON—Author, *Reluctant Burglar*

A FRIDAY AFTERNOON CLUB MYSTERY

crime

&

clutter

HOWARD
Fiction
A DIVISION OF SIMON & SCHUSTER
New York   London   Toronto   Sydney

cyndy salzmann

author of DYING TO DECORATE

Our purpose at Howard Books is to:
•*Increase faith* in the hearts of growing Christians
•*Inspire holiness* in the lives of believers
•*Instill hope* in the hearts of struggling people everywhere
Because He's coming again!

Published by Howard Books, a division of Simon & Schuster, Inc.
1230 Avenue of the Americas, New York, NY 10020

www.howardpublishing.com

HOWARD
Fiction

Crime & Clutter © 2007 by Cyndy Salzmann

In association with Janet Kobobel Grant/Books & Such Literary Agency

Library of Congress Cataloging-in-Publication Data

Salzmann, Cynthia S.
  Crime & clutter / Cyndy Salzmann.
    p. cm.
  ISBN-13: 978-1-58229-644-9 (trade paper)
  ISBN-10: 1-58229-644-8 (trade paper)
  I. Title. II. Title: Crime and clutter.
  PS3619.A446C75 2007
  813'.6—dc22   2006039392

10 9 8 7 6 5 4 3 2

HOWARD colophon is a registered trademark of Simon & Schuster, Inc.

Manufactured in the United States of America

For information regarding special discounts for bulk purchases, please contact Simon & Schuster Special Sales at 1-800-456-6798 or business@simonandschuster.com.

Edited by Ramona Cramer Tucker
Interior design by Tennille Paden
Cover design by Terry Dugan

Proverbs 10:1 is taken from *God's Word*. *God's Word* is a copyrighted work of God's Word to the Nations. Quotations are used by permission. Copyright 1995 by God's Word to the Nations. All rights reserved. Ecclesiastes 3:1–8 is taken from the *Third Millennium Bible* (TMB), *New Authorized Version*, copyright 1998. Used by permission of Deuel Enterprises, Inc., Gary, SD 57237. All rights reserved. Proverbs 18:21 is taken from *The Message*. Copyright ©1993, 1994, 1995, 1996, 2000, 2001, 2002. Used by permission of NavPress Publishing Group. Scripture quotations attributed to *NASB* are taken from the *New American Standard Bible*®. Copyright © 1960, 1962, 1963, 1968, 1971, 1972, 1973, 1975, 1977, 1995, by the Lockman Foundation. Used by permission. www.lockman.org.

This novel is a work of fiction. Names, characters, places, and incidents either are the product of the author's imagination or are used fictitiously. Any resemblance to actual events, locales, organizations, or persons, living or dead, is entirely coincidental and beyond the intent of either the author or publisher.

To Freddy,
for without your persistence, this book would not be complete.
Thank you, my dear son. Your father and I are so very
proud of the man you have become.

A WISE SON MAKES HIS FATHER HAPPY.
PROVERBS 10:1, *GOD'S WORD*

ACKNOWlEDGMENts

I am indebted to many people who helped make this book a reality.

Philis Boultinghouse and Chrys Howard of Howard Books. Without your encouragement and persistence, this book series would still be an idea—and I would still be behind on laundry.

Ramona Cramer Tucker, for her excellent editing and sweet encouragement. What a privilege it has been to partner with you!

My wonderful agent, Janet Kobobel Grant of Books & Such Literary Agency, for her advice, professionalism, enthusiasm, and honesty. You motivate me to practice my craft not somehow . . . but triumphantly.

Linda Nathan, for sharing her personal journey during the turbulent sixties and directing me toward some excellent resources.

Kelli Standish, for giving me an insider's look into the life of a collective community.

Mark Bandemer, for personal insights into Chicago city neighborhoods in, and reminiscences about, the riots during the 1968 Democratic National Convention. Watch out, Mark, the Yippies are coming!

Sergeant Clarence Contestabile, for his honesty and insight as a career police officer—particularly during the turbulent sixties and seventies.

The staff and resources of the Omaha Public Library for research assistance—again and again.

Chris, Kelsey, and the rest of the gang at Camille's, who kept my coffee cup full.

Frank Sommer III, for sharing his recipe for the best ribs I've ever tasted.

The members of the Christian Authors Network (CAN) for their encouragement, prayers, and patience.

Acknowledgments

My talented critique partners—Mary Connealy, Christy Barritt, and Anne Greene—who helped me sift the wheat from the chaff in this manuscript. You guys are the greatest!

My dear friend and fellow author Carol Umberger, for her expertise and encouragement.

My sweet and patient children—Freddy, Liz, and Anna—who pitched in on household chores to help me meet my deadline. Freddy, thanks for sharing your recipe—and for keeping me on schedule.

My supportive husband, John, for his encouragement—and help with the laundry. I love you, sweetheart!

And, of course, my own Friday Afternoon Club—Mary, Liz, Shirley, P.J., Mirm, Jean, Danette, Lorna, Deb, and Denise—for their treasured friendship. You will always be close to my heart!

Finally, but most importantly, almighty God, for allowing me to serve him with my writing.

Let the favor of the Lord our God be upon us;
And confirm for us the work of our hands.

PSALM 90:17, *NASB*

To every thing there is a season, and a time for every purpose under the heaven: a time to be born, and a time to die; a time to plant, and a time to pluck up that which is planted; a time to kill, and a time to heal; a time to break down, and a time to build up; a time to weep, and a time to laugh; a time to mourn, and a time to dance; a time to cast away stones, and a time to gather stones together; a time to embrace, and a time to refrain from embracing; a time to get, and a time to lose; a time to keep, and a time to cast away; a time to rend, and a time to sew; a time to keep silence, and a time to speak; a time to love, and a time to hate; a time of war, and a time of peace.

ECCLESIASTES 3:1–8, *Third Millennium Bible*

crime
&
clutter

chAPTER
ONE

FRESH LEMONADE

1 cup sugar

9 cups cold water

1 1/2 cups fresh lemon juice

1 tablespoon finely grated lemon peel (yellow part only)

Lemon slices and fresh mint leaves for garnish (optional)

Instructions

1. Combine sugar and 1 cup water in small saucepan over medium heat. Bring to a boil.
2. Reduce heat and simmer about 5 minutes, stirring occasionally. Remove from heat, and cool completely.
3. Combine syrup with lemon juice, peel, and remaining water.
4. Serve in a glass over ice. Garnish with a lemon slice and fresh mint, if desired.

Makes 2 1/2 quarts.

EASY CROCKPOT LEMON CHICKEN

5–6 frozen, skinless chicken breasts (bone in)

lemon pepper seasoning

2 tablespoons melted butter

Instructions

1. Season chicken breasts with lemon pepper.
2. Place in slow cooker. Pour melted butter over chicken.
3. Cover and cook on low 8–10 hours.

I have always hated guinea pigs—or any kind of rodent for that matter. So why I agreed to become one in my sixteen-year-old son's psychology experiment is still a mystery.

Perhaps it was the puppy dog look in Josh's chocolate brown eyes. Or maternal pride at being asked to do something that didn't involve cooking or laundry. Maybe I'm just a sucker, and he knows it.

Regardless of the reason, I, Elizabeth Harris—grown woman and award-winning lifestyle columnist—find myself sitting at the kitchen table with a number-two pencil clutched in each hand, poised over two blank sheets of paper.

I am supposed to simultaneously draw a circle with my right hand and a square with my left. Although I'm trying to concentrate, all I can think about is how I'd like to get my hands on the sadistic psychology teacher who thought up this inane project.

"Ready, Mom?" My freckle-faced son is standing over me—thumb cocked to click on his stopwatch.

"I guess."

In a split second, I reconsider my answer. "No! Wait! My palms are sweating. Let me wipe them off."

I rise from the chair to grab the striped dishtowel hanging from the handle of the stove.

"Come on, Mom! I've got baseball practice in thirty minutes. We've gotta get this done. My project is due Monday, and my psych teacher—"

Hot button.

A spark of parental ire temporarily replaces my nervousness at garnering a low score and having my lack of dexterity whispered about at PTA.

"Josh, is it my fault you waited until the last minute?" I say, leaning back on the counter and wiping my hands on the dishtowel.

Do all children wait until a project is in crisis mode before beginning, or am I one of the lucky mothers whose kids claim to work best under pressure?

"Mom, you're the one who's been telling me all week we'd do it later," my son reminds me. Rather smugly, I might add.

Another hot button. Insecurity sprinkled with maternal guilt. A teenager's perfect weapon.

Before I can fully explore the depths of culpability, the telephone rings. All sense of scholastic duty forgotten, my son snatches up the cordless phone from behind the microwave.

No wonder I couldn't find the phone when I needed to call John this morning.

"Oh yeah, she's here, Miz Favazza," he says in a low tone. "But she's kinda busy."

Busy! Josh would kill me if I told one of his friends he was busy and couldn't come to the phone. I hold out my hand. "Josh. Give me the phone."

Josh blows a hank of russet-colored hair out of his eyes and gives me the handset.

"I'll just be a minute." I turn away before speaking into the phone. "Hi, Marina. You're still coming over for FAC today, aren't you?"

"Yeah, I'll be there," Marina booms on the other end of the line, "but maybe a little late. That's why I'm calling."

I hear the chirp of the police radio in the background.

"Hold on a sec, Liz, will ya? Hey, Stokes! Tell Nino to quit flirting with the counter girl."

I laugh to myself. Marina is one of two female lieutenants on the Omaha, Nebraska, police department. Although very feminine with her wild black hair and perfect manicure, she can stand up to even the most macho of men.

"Okay, I'm back," she says into the phone. "Nino thinks he's God's gift to women. Give me a break. Now . . . what were we talking about?"

"You said you might be late for FAC."

"Oh yeah. I'm wrapping things up at a sting out here in the boonies."

"Sounds exciting."

"At least it's better than the duty I pulled last week at the Omaha Country Club. Try watching a bunch of aging frat boys play golf all afternoon. It's enough to drive even a patient woman like me crazy."

I catch Josh's pleading look out of the corner of my eye and hold up a finger to let him know I'll be off the phone soon.

"But this afternoon did have its highlights," continues Marina, oblivious to the teenage angst in my kitchen. "I saw Mary Alice out here paying the rent on a storage unit. In cash."

This catches my attention. "M.A. with a secret stash of stuff? I always knew those uncluttered counters were too good to be true. Did you ask her what's up?"

"No, I couldn't. I was undercover. But when I get through with her this afternoon, the queen of clutter control better fess up. Or she may have to give up that crown." Laughing, I press the end button on the handset. My humor turns sour as I spot the dreaded experiment waiting for me on the kitchen table.

●

*T*his has got to stop!"

I look up from my fourth try at completing Josh's experiment to see my normally patient husband red-faced and sweating at the door leading from the garage into the kitchen.

Granted, it's a welcome interruption from my torturous task. But what is John doing home so early?

"Wuz up, Dad?" asks my son. "You okay?"

"No. I am not okay."

I rise from the kitchen table and cross the room to place a hand on my husband's forehead. "Are you sick, sweetheart? Is that why you're home early?"

He gently brushes my hand away. "Don't worry, Liz, I'm not sick. I came home early because I knew you were having FAC. I wanted to get the kids out of your hair so you'd have plenty of time to do whatever it is you do."

"Really? You came home early for me?" I give his shoulders a squeeze. "You are so sweet!"

"Well, I try," says John, basking in my appreciation.

I can understand why he is basking. Poor guy—or should I say, guys. Most husbands have no clue about what makes a woman tick. Like how we can get absolutely ecstatic over an offer to clean the bathroom but then often greet attempts at buying us gifts with a smile that fails to mask the *What was he thinking?* in our eyes. A perfect example is the set of salad tongs shaped like bear claws that John bought me on his Alaskan fishing trip to let me know he was thinking of me.

Exactly *what* was he thinking?

But to my husband's credit, one thing he does get is my need for FAC. And his thoughtfulness in coming home early so I can enjoy the afternoon without the regular chaos of our busy home has earned him major brownie points.

So what in the world is FAC? Our family members have called it a lot of things in the past. Funky Adult Conversation. Friendship And Chocolate. Even, Fabulous After Children. The truth is far from exotic. FAC is short for Friday Afternoon Club—a group of women (Lucy, Jessie, Marina, Mary Alice, Kelly, and me) who get together on Friday afternoons for that vital shot of "girl time" that all women need but too often sacrifice.

Today is my turn to host—and my family is well aware that FAC is an important factor in keeping Mom happy. Just like the old saying: "If Mama ain't happy . . . ain't nobody happy."

My son interrupts my musings. "If you're not sick, Dad, then why is your face all red?"

John takes a deep breath, pushes a lock of sandy hair off his sweat-slicked brow, and straightens to his full height of six feet. "My face may appear to be a little red because I'm frustrated. I'm tired of people in this house borrowing my things and not putting them back."

"What did you lose now, honey?" I say in a soothing tone, my hand rubbing his shoulder.

When John delivers one of those "don't treat me like one of the kids" looks, I realize this is the wrong approach.

"I didn't *lose* anything. Someone took the garage door opener out of my car."

"The garage-door opener? You mean the controller?"

Before John can answer my question, Josh slips the stopwatch into his pocket and heads toward the door. "Gotta go! I'm late for baseball practice."

"Not so fast, young man." John blocks any hope of easy escape by placing a strong arm across the doorway. "Did you take the opener out of my car?"

"Why would I do that?"

"You didn't answer my question."

"I said I didn't take it, Dad. Why do you always blame me?"

The muscles in John's cheek begin to twitch.

Not a good sign.

Oblivious, Josh continues. "What about Katie? Why don't you ask her? She uses the car more than I do."

John's face takes on a deeper shade of red and a little bead of sweat meanders down his left cheek.

I attempt to diffuse the situation before it turns into a full-blown case of sibling rivalry, further frustrating my husband. Josh, our middle child, often feels overshadowed by his strong-willed older sister, Katie, and out-maneuvered by our precocious younger daughter, Hannah. "Now Josh, let's not bring—"

"Young man," John continues sternly, his brown eyes intense, "I'm sick and tired of hearing 'I don't know' or 'I didn't take it' whenever something is missing around this house. Someone has to know what happened to my garage-door opener, and I intend to—"

"Come on, Dad," Josh interrupts, "whaddya want me to say? I don't have it. And I'm already late for practice 'cuz Mom hates guinea pigs."

My husband shoots me a quizzical look.

I shrug. We've had many discussions about what I believe may be a vast conspiracy to pass rodents off as pets.

John obviously decides not to pursue the subject, sighs, and lowers his arm. "Fine. But this subject is not closed."

I shake my head sadly, knowing what the real problem is. My husband refuses to accept the presence of what I've come to call "the troll under the house." This ugly little pest emerges periodically with one goal—to drive unsuspecting parents crazy. He taunts us by secretly siphoning all the gas from the family car. He creates unimaginable frustration by wearing clothes that are not his—and hanging them back in our closets with mysterious stains. He is also a master at leaving dirty dishes and wet towels all over the house. If John could just learn to accept that our troll will probably get bored and move away after the kids go to college, he'd be much happier.

"Sweetheart, sit down. Let me get you something to drink."

I cross to the refrigerator to pull out a pitcher of my sugary lemonade. Perhaps an infusion of carbs will elevate both our moods.

Our younger daughter, Hannah, charges into the room, strawberry blond curls bouncing with indignation. "Mom, tell Katie to quit flicking her belly-button lint at me!"

"Katie is doing what?" I ask our eleven-year-old.

Hannah wrinkles her nose. "Mom, she is so gross! You would think that someone who is going to college next year would—"

"Just so you know, Mother," shouts my older daughter from the family room, "I would never do anything so disgusting. Hannah's trying to get me in trouble because I won't take her to the mall."

"Hannah . . . ," I warn.

"Come here, sweetie," says John, reaching an arm out to Hannah. "Do *you* know what happened to my garage-door opener? There's a trip to the mall for the first person to find it."

Once again, my poor husband is forced to use a frustrated parent's tool of last resort. Bribery. I've been there myself. More often than I care to admit. As I check on the Lemon Chicken I put in the Crockpot for dinner, I wonder what Dr. Dobson would think.

chAPTER TWO

LIZ'S CITRUS COOLER

1 (12 ounce) can frozen lemonade concentrate, thawed

1 (6 ounce) can frozen orange juice concentrate, thawed

1 lemon

1 lime

1 orange

2 liters chilled sparkling water

Instructions

1. Pour lemonade and orange juice concentrate into pitcher.
2. Wash and slice fruit, leaving the rind. Reserve a few slices to garnish the glasses. Place the rest in pitcher.
3. Add sparkling water to pitcher. Stir until thoroughly mixed.
4. Place a slice of fruit on the rim of each glass. Serve immediately over ice.

Makes 12 cups.

MARY ALICE'S PESTO CHEESECAKE

1 tablespoon butter, room temperature

2 tablespoons fine dry bread crumbs

1/2 cup plus 2 tablespoons grated Parmesan cheese

2 (8 ounce) packages cream cheese, room temperature

1 cup ricotta cheese

1/4 teaspoon salt

1/8 teaspoon cayenne pepper

3 large eggs

1/2 cup prepared pesto

paprika and basil (to sprinkle on top)

Instructions

1. Preheat oven to 325 degrees.
2. Rub 1 tablespoon butter over bottom and sides of 9-inch springform pan.
3. Mix bread crumbs and 2 tablespoons grated cheese. Coat pan with crumb mixture.
4. Using electric mixer, beat cream cheese, ricotta, remaining Parmesan, salt, and cayenne pepper in large bowl until light. Add eggs ones at a time, beating well after each addition.
5. Transfer half the mixture to medium bowl. Mix pesto into remaining half.
6. Pour pesto mixture into prepared pan. Smooth top. Carefully spoon plain mixture over pesto mixture, and smooth top. Sprinkle top of plain mixture with paprika and basil.
7. Bake until center no longer moves when pan is shaken, about 60 minutes.
8. Transfer to rack. Cool completely. Cover and refrigerate.
9. To remove from pan for serving, run a small sharp knife around sides to loosen cheesecake. Release pan sides.
10. Transfer to platter. Serve with crackers.

MARINA'S INFAMOUS GREASEBALLS

1 cup packed brown sugar

2 tablespoons Worcestershire sauce

2 cups ketchup

1 pound bacon

2 (8 ounce) cans water chestnuts

Instructions

1. Preheat oven to 375 degrees.
2. Combine brown sugar, Worcestershire sauce, and ketchup in a bowl.
3. Wrap a half slice of bacon around each water chestnut. Secure bacon with toothpick.
4. Arrange in 9x13-inch baking dish. Bake 10–15 minutes.
5. Remove from oven and drain grease from pan. Pour sauce on top.
6. Return to oven and continue baking 20–25 more minutes.

$\mathcal{A}$fter expressing both dismay and delight at the discovery of the lost garage-door opener on top of the washing machine, John whisks Hannah off to the mall. He even convinces Katie to come along. On a Friday afternoon, no less. I seem to remember her telling me that a teenager can't be caught dead with her parents on a Friday. John must have promised her a new outfit. More brownie points.

I'd love to be a fly on the register when the clerk rings up the girls' purchases. Men have no clue what a mere T-shirt and pair of worn-looking jeans with an initial stitched on the pocket can cost.

"Lord, please don't let him ask the clerk for a discount because of the frayed knee," I pray. Just the thought of the mortification on Katie's face is enough to make me shudder.

The doorbell rings, and our ever-watchful Westie charges to the front of the house to check out the intruder on *her* front porch. *Is it four o'clock and time for FAC already?*

I hear Daisy's boisterous barking and her nails clicking on the glass as she leaps at the storm door in her best imitation of the Doberman down the block. What can I say? The dog has issues. Oprah had a guest on her show the other day—the Dog Whisperer—who contends that dogs with a "big dog" complex are out of balance "spiritually." He supposedly helped Oprah's cocker spaniel regain a positive energy balance. I say, give the poor dog a break. So she wants to act like a big dog. Sometimes I like to pretend I look like Meg Ryan and can wear size 2 jeans.

Since I don't hear a voice on the porch responding to Daisy's outburst, I have a pretty good idea which member of FAC is at the door. Sweet Lucy would likely greet our feisty pup in soothing tones before slipping through the door into the foyer. Jessie usually has an organic dog treat in the pocket of her long denim skirt to gain her an easy entry. Belying her diminutive frame, Kelly would instruct Daisy in an alpha voice to

"Behave!" And Marina, no doubt about it, would bark right back—sending Daisy scurrying upstairs to hide under Hannah's bed.

That leaves Mary Alice, the most polite member of our group. Mary Alice must be waiting patiently for someone to save her from Daisy and her big-dog complex.

I shove evidence of my pitiful results from Josh's behavioral-psychology experiment into the kitchen drawer—still wondering what demented researcher thinks up these sadistic experiments. As I walk to the door, I conclude the project must be a scheme to get back at parents who toss a box of Twinkies into their kid's backpack instead of sending *real* classroom treats.

I can't suppress a self-satisfied smile when I reach the door. I was right. Standing on the porch is Mary Alice, perfectly attired for the balmy spring day in a darling pair of black capri pants embroidered with a pattern of colorful little flip-flops. Her sweater and matching tee are the exact shade of blue of one of the tiny shoes. As always, her makeup is perfect, her haircut stylish—and without dark roots marring her ash-blond highlights. She's holding a tray of her famous Pesto Cheesecake.

She probably even shaved her legs.

"Hi Lizzie," she says. "Am I early?"

Always.

"Not at all, M.A. Come on in." I crack open the door while trying to hold my leaping canine back with my leg. "You know, after all these years, you don't have to ring the bell. Just come on in."

Our FAC group has been getting together on Friday afternoons for more than eleven years now. We know one another the way only good friends can. This is a group where letting your hair down is not only encouraged, it's in our mythical bylaws . . . along with a list of banned words such as *diet, carbs, workout,* and *scrapbooking.*

To the majority of women, the reasons behind banning the words *diet, carbs,* and *workout* are obvious. The rationale behind banning *scrapbooking* is a bit more subtle. All of us in FAC would love to have gorgeous up-to-date scrapbooks for our children. But only two of us do. Kelly and—big surprise—Mary Alice. The FAC meeting that prompted our decision to banish *scrapbooking* or associated terms from our approved list of conversation topics is seared into my memory . . .

●

I went to a Stop 'n' Crop yesterday," said Kelly as we filled each other in on our activities during the past week. "It was a blast—and I got a lot done."

Marina slapped the table with her hand. "You were stopped by a cop? Tell me who it was, and I'll fry him like bacon."

Jessie laughed. "I'm sure you would, Rina. But don't worry. Kelly's talking about a *crop*—not a cop. There's nothing illegal about it."

"Just annoying," I mumbled.

Marina shot me a puzzled look. I rolled my eyes, not wanting to admit the real reason for my annoyance. The green-eyed monster. Lucy sat down at the table. "Okay, I'll bite. What's a crop?"

"It's a way to catch up on your scrapbooks," explained Mary Alice. "You bring your photos and scrapbooking supplies and spend the day putting together pages. I got our entire trip to Worlds of Fun done the last time I did a crop."

I moaned. "Why in the world would you do that, M.A.? I do my best to block a day at an amusement park from my memory. Standing in a forty-five-minute line for a ride that makes my stomach lurch is not a memory I want to relive."

Marina snorted. "Lightweight!"

Although I succeeded in changing the subject, I would have killed to have a shelf of neatly catalogued memory books chronicling the milestones of our family life. The kinds of scrapbooks my children would pull down to spend hours gushing, "Remember when we . . ."

Instead I had shoeboxes.

Lots of shoeboxes.

Shoeboxes brimming over with unorganized photos. Stuffed in the hall closet along with several brown grocery sacks overflowing with mementos of birthdays, vacations, and special events. I was saving these things to one day affix to acid-free paper with witty journal entries and the ubiquitous embellishments.

Someday. When I had time.

"Anyway," Kelly continued, sounding annoyed at being interrupted, "they have some great new diecuts at the scrapbook store."

"Really?" Mary Alice leaned forward. "I end up using my Coluzzle most of the time."

Lucy peered at me from across the table. "Marina, Liz has that look on her face. Do you still keep Snickers in your glove compartment for emergencies?"

"I'm on it!" Marina jumped up and headed to the front door.

I sigh. "I know how important it is to kids to preserve family memories. But I never seem to have the time."

"I know how you feel, Lizzie." Jess, who was sitting on the other side of me, scooped up a handful of roasted almonds. "I have a baby book put together for Sarah, but things got more hectic after Ryan came along, and I got behind. In fact, I barely have any snapshots of the two youngest."

"That's nothing," I added. "I can't even tell which kid is which in the pictures."

"If you can't tell, then they won't know either," said Marina, tossing a bag of bite-sized chocolate bars on the table.

Mary Alice and Kelly exchanged a horrified look.

"What if I write the names of kids under pictures and they figure out later it's not them? They could be traumatized," I moaned.

"And headed straight for a spot on Dr. Phil." Kelly stared at me with wide eyes.

This was when Lucy suggested we add *scrapbooking* to our list of banned words. Marina seconded the motion with a mouth full of Snickers. It passed 4–2 . . .

●

I finally scoop up my treacherous terrier to allow Mary Alice to come through the door. Most dogs cover their master's face with wet kisses. My squirming pet lays a long scratch down my neck in an attempt to break free from my grasp. I make a note to check on the possibility of declawing this dog that I'm now convinced must be part cat.

"Am I the first one here?" Mary Alice asks as we walk down the hall to the kitchen.

A familiar voice comes from the kitchen. "You wish!"

I smile. Marina must have slipped in the back door. Typical.

"I could smell the garlic in that cheesecake on the next block." Marina pulls out a chair and plops down at my kitchen table. "You think I'm gonna let you two low-carb fanatics alone with such a masterpiece? In ten minutes all that'll be left are whole-grain crackers."

Mary Alice sets the platter on the table and removes the plastic wrap. The amber and green design on the serving dish accentuates the golden cheesecake. Fresh basil and red peppers are artfully arranged as a garnish.

"Let me get you a knife for that." I open my cluttered utensil drawer and root around. "I think I have some crackers in the pantry too."

"Don't bother, Lizzie. I have it covered." Mary Alice pulls a box of crackers and a small bubble-wrapped spreader from her Lands' End zippered tote bag.

As usual, M.A. has thought of everything.

"Wait a minute." Marina peers across the table as Mary Alice unwraps the serving utensil. The handle is shaped like a pink flamingo. "Isn't that mine?"

"Yes. You left it at my house last week."

"So now I'm gonna have to wash it again? If I would've known I was going to have extra dishes, I wouldn't have gone to all this trouble to make a pan of my Greaseballs."

Mary Alice and I exchange a glance.

"Greaseballs?" I ask.

"Yeah, they're in the oven. They're best nice and hot. That way the grease doesn't start to congeal."

Sounds delicious.

"You put something called *Greaseballs* in my oven?" Even though I have no idea what a Greaseball might be, I know from our many years of friendship that *Marina* and *cooking* are two words that are far from compatible. As if the appliance could read my thoughts, smoke begins to stream from the oven vent on top of the stove.

"What—" Marina gets up from the table.

Mary Alice looks frantically around the kitchen. "Liz, where's your fire extinguisher?"

"I-I don't have—" I sputter.

The piercing squeal of the smoke alarm sounds, prompting Daisy to start barking from the top of the stairs. Probably too scared to come down after hearing Marina's voice.

"Baking soda then," shouts Mary Alice over the commotion. She rips open the door of my pantry, scanning the shelves. "Where do you keep it?"

Baking soda? Why would she want . . . ?

"Liz, snap out of it!" Marina grabs my shoulders. "We've got a fire here!"

"A fire . . . ?"

Marina snatches up the cordless phone from the counter and punches in the familiar emergency number—911.

I whirl around to help Mary Alice. Too late.

She has already spied the familiar orange box of baking soda behind the tower of canned tuna no one in my family will eat. No matter how many times I explain the health benefits of Omega 3. She grabs the box, expertly rips off the top, dons the oven mitt hanging above the stove (the one that is only for decoration), and yanks open the oven door. A rush of heat, smoke, and a few flames pour out. Mary Alice stands back and dumps the baking soda inside the oven to put out the fire.

Once the flames have been doused, she leans back, wide-eyed and panting. "It's out."

"Yeah, but look at my Greaseballs."

I give Marina a withering look, but before I can say anything, a siren wails in the distance.

"That's the fire department. I'll handle 'em." Marina heads down the hall to the front door.

As a cop, Marina knows a lot of people in public safety. She feels it's her sacred duty to act as a buffer between the trained professionals and the "amateurs" (meaning anyone without a badge) whenever possible. Since it would be just my luck that there's some obscure city code requiring a fire extinguisher in the kitchen, I'm grateful for Marina's intervention.

●

*A*lthough our resident professional was able to keep the Omaha Fire Department from chopping through my front door and the rescue squad from sweeping in with a stretcher, Marina didn't do a thing to prevent the lecture the fireman gave me about the danger of grease fires.

There's nothing more humiliating than having a tall, physically fit man lecturing you about cooking food with high fat content. The only other thing I remember about the conversation was the coupon for two dollars off a small fire extinguisher and the grin Marina flashed over her shoulder as she walked the firefighters back to their truck.

Why me? Why are my FACs always so eventful? . . .

●

There was the time Daisy got into a box of chocolate and started vomiting all over the house during one of my turns to host FAC. After Jess told me chocolate was poisonous to canines, I called the vet. He suggested I give Daisy hydrogen peroxide to induce more vomiting.

"But I want the vomiting to *stop*," I tried to explain.

The vet's response was very calm. "Then you may have a dead dog tonight."

Hannah, who happened to be listening on the extension, gasped. Needless to say, I got out the brown bottle of hydrogen peroxide. And the carpet cleaner.

Another eventful FAC occurred when Kelly convinced me she could add highlights to my hair at a fourth of the cost my stylist was charging. The resulting pumpkin-colored stripes caused me to weep every time I passed a mirror. And Marina's suggestion to try out for a punk rock band did not help.

But the most memorable FAC was when the outside valve from our sprinkler system burst due to cold weather. I got the news from six-year-old Taylor, who lives next door.

"Um, Mrs. Harris . . ."

"Yes, Taylor, what can I do for you?" I cracked open the front door.

"Um, there's this . . ."

I smiled, encouraging her to continue in my best imitation of Mrs. Brady. "If you are selling Christmas wreaths to raise money for your soccer team again, put me down for—"

"Uh, no. It's just that there's all this water squirting out the side of your house."

"Water? From my house?"

"You gotta see it, Mrs. Harris! It looks like a fountain. Only sideways."

It took a tour of my cluttered basement and six calls to John to get the water main shut off. The result was no water for the entire house until he could get home to repair the sprinkler valve. I announced to my friends that they better watch their liquid intake because the toilet could only be flushed once.

Marina's comment was typical. "When it's yellow, let it mellow. When it's brown . . ."

Memorable.

●

*M*ary Alice has already removed Marina's ruined Greaseballs—supposedly bacon-wrapped water chestnuts in a brown-sugar sauce—from my oven. It was hard to tell what they were with all the baking soda now sopping up the grease and forming little gritty lumps.

"Liz, can I set the oven rack on the back deck?"

"Don't worry about it, M.A. I'll clean up the mess later."

"It's no problem. Once the oven cools, we can vacuum most of the gunk from the bottom. Then you can run the self-cleaner overnight."

I sigh. Why argue with a domestic diva? "Sure go ahead. Put the rack on the back deck. Dustbuster or Wind Tunnel?"

She smiles. "Your Wind Tunnel will do a better job."

That means digging out the attachments too. I'm going to kill Marina and her Greaseballs.

●

*L*eaving Mary Alice in the kitchen, vacuuming, wiping, and humming, I decide to see what's taking Marina so long with the firemen in the front yard. As soon as I step on the porch, I am accosted by Kelly, another member of FAC.

"Liz, calm down. Breathe deeply and tell me exactly what happened."

Kelly is one of those people who likes to organize things—particularly other people's lives. She's only five foot two, but like a firecracker, she packs a lot of power in a small package. And trust me, no one wants to set her off.

"Really, Kel, it ended up being no big deal. Marina—"

Kelly purses her lips. "I should have known Marina was involved. Did this have anything to do with cooking?"

"Well, actually—"

"Kelly, stop badgering Liz," interrupts Jessie, sweeping up the porch steps in a bright skirt with broomstick pleats that graze the top of her Birkenstock sandals. "Lizzie, are you all right? I saw the rescue squad pull away." She puts a protective arm around my shoulder.

"I'm fine. But I wish the fire department would leave. The crew already checked the house."

"They *are* causing quite a stir in the neighborhood." Lucy, the sixth member of our group, completes the tight circle on my front porch. She nods at the house across the street.

Mrs. Robinson, self-appointed chairwoman of the neighborhood grapevine, is peeking through the heavy, gold draperies that cover her picture window. I wave as red blotches begin to bloom on my neck.

What was it Scarlett O'Hara used to say?

"I'd rather not think about it now," I say out loud. "Tomorrow is another day."

At times like this, I wish I were from the South.

●

There was a fire in here?" Jessie asks as we step into the kitchen. "Where's all the mess?"

"Mary Alice . . ." I begin.

Jessie smiles and leans down so her long, dark brown waves shield one side of her face. "Enough said."

Kelly walks up behind us, sniffing the air. "I can barely smell smoke."

Mary Alice steps into the kitchen from the garage and closes the door behind her. "It was such a nice day that I opened the window and turned on the whole house fan to pull the smoke out. I hope that was okay, Liz?"

"Of course, but—"

Kelly picks up a bowl of clear liquid from the counter. "What's this? It smells like vinegar."

"It is," explains Mary Alice. "Vinegar takes away odors. Your family won't even know there's been a fire, Liz."

I smile, knowing full well that I intend to tell them *all* about the incident. I might even dig out a little soot to rub on my face from the vacuum bag that I'm sure Mary Alice has already changed and put in the garbage. Maybe if my family sees I've had a rough afternoon, they'll be less whiny tonight.

No one knows the meaning of carpe diem like a mother. *Seize the day!*

●

*F*inally I am settled at the kitchen table with my five friends—smearing my third whole-grain cracker with Mary Alice's delicious Pesto Cheesecake. This is what FAC is all about. Fun. Friends. And, of course, food.

"So, Marina, does Jeff know you're so buddy-buddy with the brave men of the Omaha Fire Department?" teases Kelly.

"Hey little girl, Jeff is a man who is not threatened by my career."

Bravado is Marina's middle name, but we all know her relationship with local contractor/farmer Jeff Taylor is deepening. In fact, Lucy had a close-up view of their relationship while Jeff supervised the renovation of her house in nearby Tredway. And, she said she wouldn't be surprised if Jeff turns out to be *the one.*

"Actually, I wanted to ask them how a bust we made earlier today at Storage Unlimited ended up. The fire department went in to clean up after my team left."

Mary Alice rises from the table. "I'm going to have some more of Liz's Citrus Cooler. Anyone else need a refill?"

I look up. Mary Alice seems a little pale. I always knew cleaning was hazardous to your health.

"Sit. I'll get it, M.A."

Mary Alice puts her hand on my shoulder. "No, you sit, Lizzie. You've had enough excitement this afternoon.

I could get used to being waited on.

Jess turns to Marina. "Isn't Storage Unlimited the place out near Elkhorn? That's where Michael stores our boat."

"Yeah, that's the one." Marina snags another cheese-laden cracker.

"Was there a burglary?" I eye Marina's cracker, calculating carbs to determine if I should have another one.

"You know I don't work on B&Es anymore, Liz. Remember? I moved to Vice."

"How could I have forgotten?" I raise an eyebrow in her direction. "I was your shopping buddy for undercover hookerwear."

Marina snorts. "That was a trip I won't forget. You shoulda saw prim Lizzie when I tried on a micromini."

Kelly shakes her head. "You guys couldn't stay on track if it were fenced. Come on, Marina, tell us what was going down at the storage place."

"We busted a meth lab out in Douglas County—and Storage Unlimited is where they were stashing their supplies."

"You're kidding!" says Kelly. "I just went to a continuing-ed class called The Drug Lab Next Door. It was about how easy it is to make crystal meth and how popular it's getting to be among high-school and college kids."

"Not only with kids," adds Lucy, slipping a stray lock of her blond pageboy behind an ear. "One of the women staying at Locust Hill is married to a guy hooked on crystal meth."

Hearing Lucy mention Locust Hill buoys my spirits. We are so proud of how she has taken the Civil War–era home she inherited from her mother and turned it into a refuge for battered women and their children. Lucy told us recently that the transformation of Locust Hill last fall now seems less about renovating the old house and more about God's way of helping her emerge from a dark period in her life.

"How many families do you have staying at Locust Hill these days?" I ask.

"Right now, we are bursting at the seams with five families. And it seems most of the problems are tied to addictions."

"That's really common among batterers," says Kelly. "Paranoia and violent behavior really increase on meth."

I shudder. "It's scary to think drug dealers are operating so close to where we live."

Marina snorts. "If you only knew what goes on in your backyard. Which reminds me . . ." Marina winks at me across the table and calls over her shoulder to Mary Alice, in the kitchen, "By the way, M.A., what were you doing out at Storage Unlimited this morning?"

The only response was Mary Alice's gasp as the pitcher of Citrus Cooler slipped from her hand. Followed by the deafening sound of glass shattering on the ceramic tile floor.

chapter THREE

COMFORT CHOCOLATE

2 pounds white chocolate

4 ounces milk chocolate

1 (12 ounce) package semisweet chocolate chips

24 ounces roasted pecans or almonds

Instructions

1. Put all ingredients in slow cooker. Cook on high 1 hour. Do not stir.
2. Switch slow cooker to low setting. Cook 1 hour longer, stirring every 15 minutes.
3. Drop chocolate by spoonfuls on waxed paper. Let cool.
4. Store in tightly covered container.

Makes about 3 dozen comfort chocolates.

FIVE-MINUTE FUDGE

2 tablespoons butter

2/3 cup evaporated milk

1 2/3 cups sugar

1/2 teaspoon salt

2 cups miniature marshmallows

1 1/2 cups semisweet chocolate chips

1 teaspoon vanilla

1/2 cup chopped pecans or walnuts (optional)

Instructions

1. Combine butter, milk, sugar, and salt in medium pan.
2. Bring to a boil over medium heat. Cook 4–5 minutes, stirring constantly.
3. Remove from heat. Stir in marshmallows, chips, vanilla, and nuts (if desired).
4. Beat with a spoon until marshmallows melt and mixture is thoroughly combined.
5. Pour into an 8-inch square, foil-lined pan. Let cool.
6. When set, cut into squares.

$\mathcal{J}$essie went to bandage a cut on Mary Alice's hand in my upstairs bathroom while Kelly supervised the cleanup of the mess in the kitchen. She had Lucy using thick layers of newspaper to soak up the sugary, amber liquid and bundle up the larger glass shards to prevent injury by unsuspecting trash collectors. I grabbed a broom to finish off the job.

"No, Liz, don't use that," says Kelly, pointing to my broom. "Bread works better."

I stop midsweep. "Did you say bread?"

"Of course. You do have a loaf of bread around here, don't you?"

I point. "In the drawer, but—"

"Is it fresh?" Kelly opens the drawer and sifts through the assortment of bread and rolls.

I pray she doesn't find anything green.

"I don't see what the age of my bread has to do with any of this."

Marina laughs. "This is rich! 'Martha' here doesn't know that the best way to get up slivers of glass is with a slice of bread. You boycotting Heloise, too, these days?"

Since I'm the author of a weekly lifestyle column in our local newspaper, my friends tease me about my reputation in Omaha as the local domestic diva. They know better. I recently came clean with my readers by admitting that I don't have all the answers to their homemaking dilemmas. And, unlike the unsinkable Martha Stewart, I couldn't dress a strawberry in a chocolate tuxedo if my life depended on it.

I even changed the name of my column from "The Lovely Life" to "Loving Life!" to reinforce my desire to provide practical solutions for *real* life. Unfortunately, some readers have taken awhile to accept this new direction. I still receive e-mails each week asking for advice on dealing with water rings on wood furniture. Regrettably, they don't appear to be amused by my suggestion to cover them with a tablecloth or potted plant.

Although I love Marina dearly, her question and Kelly's smug grin irritate me. It's been a long afternoon—beginning with being drafted as Josh's guinea pig, the grease fire, and now the mystery with Mary Alice. Not to mention the sticky mess all over my floor. As my mother used to warn when she had reached her limit, "I am in no mood."

I am extremely grateful that Lucy speaks up before I do something I'll regret with the broom I'm clutching.

"Honestly, I have no idea what you're talking about either." Lucy pushes her five-foot-nine frame up from the sticky floor.

Kelly pulls a loaf of bread from the deep drawer next to the stove. "Here it is. I knew you'd have white bread, Liz."

Warranted or not, I feel the sting of judgment for having food my health-conscious friends say has the nutritional value of cardboard. "For your information, that's a new product. It's a whole-grain white bread."

"Whatever." Kelly undoes the twist tie and takes out a soft, white slice. She squats and presses it to the tile floor. "See? The bread picks the slivers right up."

Looking at the tiny glistening shards clinging to the bread, I have to admit that her unorthodox method is working quite well. "Hmmm."

Kelly tosses the sparkly slice of bread in the garbage can. "Don't just stand there gawking, people. Grab a slice and start mopping."

●

*N*ow this is something I've never seen before," Jess says, grinning, as she walks into the kitchen with a freshly bandaged Mary Alice.

The sight of Kelly, Lucy, Marina, and me scooting around the floor on our haunches has to look a little strange. Especially since our cleaning tools are slices of bread. I'm surprised she and M.A. didn't call the fire department back to check for fumes that might have prompted this bizarre behavior.

I stand up, my knees creaking. "Don't ask. I think it's way past time to dig into the chocolate."

"Liz, I'm so sorry for making such a mess." Mary Alice's normally even-toned complexion is splotched with red. "You should have let me clean—"

I put up my hand to stop her from speaking. "Don't say another word. You've already cleaned my kitchen once today, thanks to Marina the Menace."

Marina ignores my comment and tosses a slice of bread into the trash. "Besides, this gave us a chance to teach Martha here some new tricks. When you put this tip in your column, Lizzie, be sure to spell my name right."

I shoot Marina a blistering look. "I'll be back in a minute. It's definitely time to break out my chocolate stash."

None of my friends ask why I have my own "stash" of chocolate. No explanation is needed. They are all mothers too. Chocolate, or any sweets for that matter, vanish into thin air in a home occupied by children. No matter how many warning labels a mother places on it:

Do Not Eat without Written Permission!
Stop! Eating This Candy Will Result in Immediate Restriction for an Indeterminate Length of Time.

Even, *Eat This and You DIE!* fails to keep away sticky fingers. I've resorted to hiding my chocolate treats in a place my children would never consider looking. The cleaning-supplies cabinet.

●

The six of us are gathered around the picnic table on my flagstone patio, passing a platter containing my two favorite chocolate concoctions. Both are simple to prepare, making them even more delectable.

Our FAC motto is, "When life gets sticky, dip it in chocolate." And by the expression on Mary Alice's tearstained face, I realize this is one of those sticky situations that requires a healthy dose of the cocoa-bean elixir.

As usual, Marina breaks the silence. "M.A., what gives? I've been a cop long enough to know that red face isn't because you dropped a pitcher. I wouldn't be surprised if you had an extra in the trunk of your car."

"It was an accident, Marina," I say. "And I've always hated that pitcher anyway. I got it as a wedding gift from a neighbor who used to keep all the balls that went into his yard when I was growing up. I wished he would have given me back the balls and kept the pitcher."

Mary Alice dabs her eyes with a tissue. "I'm going to replace your pitcher, Liz. I don't want to hear any arguments."

"M.A., it's really not necessary—"

Mary Alice puts her hand up to silence me and turns to Marina. "And Marina, I prefer to drop the whole subject."

That'll never fly in this group.

Mary Alice's words are like throwing a pound of bacon into a pack of hungry dogs. Once they get a tooth on a tasty tidbit, they won't let go until the last dog dies.

Marina persists as if she hasn't even heard Mary Alice. With her dark eyes boring down on M.A., my backyard begins to feel like an interrogation room.

"So if it isn't the pitcher, what's up?" Marina demands. "You had that deer-in-the-headlights look when I mentioned the drug bust. Something's obviously got your undies in a bundle."

Jess puts her arm around Mary Alice's shoulder and gives her a little squeeze. "Back off, Marina. M.A. already said she doesn't want to talk about it."

Jess may as well have been speaking to a brick wall. Not that I'm not dying to know what's going on. I just don't want to act like it.

"Don't be embarrassed," interjects Kelly, who is sitting on Mary Alice's other side. "Even kids from great families can make poor choices and get involved in drugs. I can help you nip this in the bud right—"

"Kelly," interrupts Mary Alice with a flash of parental indignation in her green eyes, "my kids don't do drugs."

"Then I can check into some good counseling for you and Craig—"

Mary Alice rubs her temples. "You've got it all wrong. My family is not involved with drugs. I mean, not right now . . ."

Lucy reaches across the picnic table to rest her hand on Mary Alice's. "Sweetie, why didn't you tell us what you were going through?"

Mary Alice looks up. "No, that's not what I meant. This is not about Craig or the kids. Okay? It has to do with a distant family member. And, as I said, I prefer not to talk about it."

Marina snorts. "That's not an option."

Mary Alice's jaw drops. After all these years, you'd think she'd know it's useless to try and thwart Marina or Kelly when they're onto a scent.

"You might as well give in now. These two will dog you until you do." I pass Mary Alice the plate of chocolate confections. "Maybe this will ease the pain."

Mary Alice waves away the chocolate. Now I know this is serious.

"I realize you all mean well, and I appreciate it. Truly. But this is something I don't want to talk about."

"Yes, you do," Kelly persists. "You may not realize it, but you do."

Mary Alice covers her face with slender, manicured hands. Lucy, Jess, and I exchange a knowing look. Doesn't this poor dear understand she's not a match for the dynamic duo? Especially when they've decided to tag-team?

"Fine." Mary Alice sighs. "It's not that big of a deal. I've been storing some family memorabilia that I haven't had time to go through yet."

Kelly shakes her head. "Doesn't add up."

"Keep going." Marina is in full cop persona, her intense black eyes never leaving M.A.'s face.

The tension is so thick that even I am getting rattled. I bite my tongue to keep from blurting out a confession or two of my own.

I admit it! My library books are overdue!

Book me! There are dust bunnies behind the television!

And yes, I left the garden hose unrolled. Again!

Mary Alice takes a deep "cleansing" breath and slowly blows it out. At least one of us is getting some use out of all that deep breathing we learned in Lamaze class. It only took one contraction in active labor before my bravado about natural childbirth dissolved and I shouted for the anesthesiologist.

"As I keep trying to tell you, it's *not* a big deal. The storage unit contains the personal effects of a relative who died last year."

I lean forward, my reporter instincts shifting into high gear. "I don't remember you telling us about anyone who died. Who was it?"

Another deep breath. "A relative from the O'Brien side who I hardly knew. A friend had his effects shipped from California about six months ago. I had it delivered directly to the storage unit and haven't had a chance to go through it. That's all there is to it."

"Still not buying it." Kelly's eyes are fixed on Mary Alice like a kid's on the last Twinkie in the box.

"Me either," adds Marina. "If you had your way, procrastination would be a punishable offense."

Mary Alice takes a sip of water from her glass. "I knew I should have just left his things in California."

"First of all, *whose* things?" asks Marina.

"And *what* things?" adds Kelly.

Mary Alice gives Jessie one of those "aren't you going to help me here?" looks.

Jess shrugs. "You might as well face the inevitable, M.A. If you don't, Marina will be on the phone setting up a stakeout in the interest of friendship."

"You bet your French manicure I will!" Marina props her elbows on the table, hands folded, showing off her meticulous acrylic nails to full advantage.

Lucy laughs. "She's right, M.A. And I wouldn't be surprised if Kelly's probably already plotting how to get you on that reality TV show. You know, the one called *Intervention*."

"Hold on a minute. You're acting like Marina and I are the meddling twosome. What about our resident journalist here?" Kelly cocks her thumb at me. "She's like a cyber PI with Google as her sidekick."

I gasp. "You think I'd Google one of my dearest friends?"

"In a New York minute," says Jess.

For the first time since the river of Citrus Cooler gushed through my kitchen, Mary Alice smiles. "Okay, I give up."

"Smart girl." Marina stretches back on two legs of her chair and rests her feet on a nearby planter. "Let's hear it."

Mary Alice looks down at the table and rubs her temples. "Last spring I received a phone call from one of my dad's old friends telling me my father had died."

All of us lean forward—including Marina, whose chair makes a *crack* on the flagstone as the legs come down. "Your *father?*"

"You didn't say a thing, M.A.," says Lucy, sorrow in her blue eyes.

I feel terrible. If there is anyone you can depend on to be there when you need her, it's Mary Alice. But when she'd needed us, we weren't there to return the favor.

"Why didn't you tell us?" I ask.

"I found out just after Lucy's mom had died, and I didn't want to make a fuss." With misty eyes, Mary Alice focuses on Lucy across the table. "I mean, you had lost your husband *and* your mom. I couldn't begin to imagine the pain you were going through. Besides, my dad and I weren't really close. He . . . he was . . ." The tear that slides down Mary Alice's cheek fills in the blanks. She reaches for a Kleenex from the box on the table.

Jess leans over to give her a hug. "Oh, sweetie."

Questions swirl through my mind. My memory is usually a little foggy, but I swear that Mary Alice has joked more than once about having an overprotective father.

Kelly, who's been uncharacteristically silent, jumps in. "I must be missing something here. I thought your father lived in Rock Port with your mom—not California."

"Did he and your mom split up?" persists Marina.

"Yes—and no." Mary Alice snatches another tissue from the box. "It's all very complicated. Can we talk about this another time?"

"No!"

The conversation stops as everyone stares, open-mouthed, at me.

Did I just say that?

Even I can't believe it. "I mean . . ."

Jess breaks the tension with her gentle smile. "We all know what you mean, Lizzie. And the rest of us are thinking the same thing."

I mouth a silent "thank you" to Jess and turn to Mary Alice. "You don't have to—Ouch!"

Marina cuts me off with a swift kick under the table.

Lucy reaches across the table to take Mary Alice's hands in her own. "We all know life doesn't fit in neat little boxes. Whatever it is, we'll understand. And you know we'll be here for you."

"But I haven't been honest with you—or Craig. Maybe even with myself." Mary Alice withdraws her hands from Lucy's and swipes at a tear. The red splotches begin to flower on her neck again. "It's like my life has been this flimsy house of cards. And now it's all starting to cave in on me."

"So let us help you pick them up. One at a time."

Kelly's caring tone takes me by surprise. For as long as I've known her, Kelly's been a doer—and has the habit of mowing down anything or anyone who gets in her way. I've always thought that's probably what makes her such an effective therapist. No pity parties with Kelly. I've heard her say on more than one occasion, "Life's hard. Learn to deal with it."

That's also the reason I've hesitated to seek Kelly's counsel in the past. I enjoy a good pity party. In fact, with some good dark chocolate and my favorite quilt, it's not a bad way to spend an afternoon.

But before I rush to get Mary Alice my "poor me" quilt, I notice her looking gratefully at Kelly and realize how alike they are. Mary Alice is a doer too. She's probably never even *entertained* the idea of indulging in a pity party. Kelly understands what someone like Mary Alice needs. A plan of action.

"Let's start with what's in the storage unit." Kelly's back to true form. Making a list. "What's keeping you from going through your dad's stuff?"

chAPTER FOUR

BLUEBERRY PANCAKES

2 cups flour

2 eggs, beaten

2 cups milk

2 tablespoons sugar

2 teaspoons baking powder

1/2 teaspoon salt

1/2 teaspoon vanilla

1 tablespoon melted butter

Blueberries (as many as you like!)

Instructions

1. Blend flour, eggs, milk, sugar, baking powder, and salt in large mixing bowl.
2. Stir in vanilla and melted butter.
3. Pour 1/4 cup of batter onto hot, greased griddle. Sprinkle each pancake with several blueberries. Flip when edges around pancake look dry.
4. Serve piping hot with butter and syrup.

Makes approximately 14–16 pancakes.

CINNAMON-SUGARED BACON

1 pound bacon, not thick-sliced, room temperature

1 1/4 cups brown sugar

2 teaspoons cinnamon

Instructions

1. Preheat oven to 350 degrees.
2. Mix brown sugar and cinnamon together. Thoroughly coat each slice of bacon.
3. Arrange on broiler pan in oven. Bake until bacon is crisp, about 15–20 minutes.

Tip: Watch closely when baking so the sugar doesn't burn. It can happen quickly!

SPARKLING JUICE

1 part chilled juice (my favorite is pineapple/mango)

1 part chilled ginger ale

Instructions

1. Mix equal parts juice and ginger ale in a stemmed glass.
2. Garnish with a maraschino cherry and a paper umbrella.

I decide to bring John breakfast in bed this morning. I enjoy surprising him with this treat every once in a while "just because." But today I have an ulterior motive.

I need someone to talk to about FAC yesterday. After all, it ended up being the most memorable FAC in our history. No . . . maybe the second most memorable. Nothing could beat the FAC at Jess's house four years ago . . .

●

*S*o Jess had caved, I thought, unable to suppress a bit of smugness, after seeing the Air Duct Pro truck in her driveway as I walked next door for our weekly FAC meeting. It seemed like one of those big, noisy trucks showed up in a different neighbor's driveway each week—poised to suck all the mold, fungus, and miscellaneous, but nevertheless disgusting, organisms from the ductwork. All because of peer pressure to clean something you couldn't even see.

But not me. I wasn't going to fold. No matter how many before and after "Duct Cam" videos my friends felt compelled to share with me, I vowed not to be intimidated by this latest scheme of the duct-cleaning services—a fiber-optic camera that workers fish through the bowels of the house to prove that the hundreds of dollars they charge is a small price to pay for saving you from what "lurks beyond the vents."

Although I cringed at the thought of microscopic organisms lying in wait in my ducts—ready to leap out and infect my family while we slept—I wasn't about to give in to air-quality hysteria. My mom never had her air ducts cleaned. And that from a woman who was such a fuss-budget when I was growing up that lemon oil was listed under staples on the grocery list.

"So what do you think they'll find?" I whispered to Jess as we stood in her front hall and watched the Hispanic technician remove one of the floor vents.

"No idea. Maybe this is where all the mates to our socks ended up."

I laughed. "Or a graveyard for missing plastic container lids."

After getting the okay from his partner in the basement, the technician fished what appeared to be an oversized bottlebrush through the vent.

"*¡Qué asco!*" he swore.

Jess laughed. "Well, at least he's honest."

"Why? What'd he say?"

Jess cupped her hand across her mouth to whisper. "He said, 'How disgusting!' Poor guy, he probably doesn't know I speak Spanish."

Poor guy, my foot.

Now I was even more convinced about my wisdom in keeping the duct patrol out from my home. The last thing I needed was some guy dissing my ventilation system. With two teenagers in the house and one ready to "cross over to the dark side," I had more than enough to keep me awake at night.

Jess took my arm. "Come on. Everybody's in the kitchen. Andy's showing off his science project."

Andy, Jess's youngest child, was a pint-sized Marlin Perkins, intent on introducing us all to his own version of Mutual of Omaha's *Wild Kingdom.*

I could imagine what was waiting for me in the kitchen. "Does this involve white mice again? You know how I feel about—"

A bloodcurdling shriek erupted from the basement, followed by the *clang* of metal and a disturbing crash.

"*¡Hombre de Dios!*" The technician working on the floor vent jumped up and raced down the stairs.

I knew I should have taken Spanish!

Before I could ask Jess to translate, Marina charged into the family room, her hand on the gun beneath her denim jacket.

"Stay here—and out of my way," she ordered, peering around the basement door like a wild-haired version of Olivia on *Law & Order: SVU* before disappearing down the steps.

By this time, Mary Alice, Lucy, Kelly, and a wide-eyed Andy had rushed into the family room.

"What's going on?" asked Lucy, her hand to her chest as if to calm a pounding heart.

"Should I call 911?" Mary Alice picked up the cordless phone from an end table.

Jess looked more than a little rattled as she pulled curly-headed Andy close to her. "I don't know. Maybe I should—"

"Kelly!" I hissed as she made a beeline to the stairs. "Marina said to stay up here."

Without a word, Kelly shot me *the look* over her shoulder. The same look Katie used to communicate, *And your point is . . . ?*

I *really* hated that look. Katie knew from experience that disrespectful words would get her grounded. But I had trouble meting out punishment for *the look*. Consequently, she'd perfected it. Obviously, so had Kelly.

"*¡Es dragón! Dragón!*" the technician yelled as he charged to the top of the stairs, forcing Kelly to jump back from the doorway.

"*¿Dragón?*" Jess approached the frantic workman, Andy in tow.

"*¡Sí, dragón!*" The man pointed repeatedly down the stairs.

Andy pushed past Jess in an attempt to head to the basement. His baggy shorts and oversized tee made him look a lot like the posters of the "skater dudes" Jess told us he had plastered all over his bedroom. "Tiki! Mom, I bet they found Tiki!"

Jess grabbed the back of his striped T-shirt like a mother lion reining in her cub. "Not so fast, mister."

"But Mom—"

"*¡Sí, dragón!*" The man continued to gesture wildly.

Jess put her hand up in an attempt to quiet the technician and squatted down to Andy's eye level. "Sweetheart, Tiki's been missing for almost three months now. We've already talked about what probably happened after he got out of his tank."

Oh no . . . I do not want to hear this.

I knew from past experience that Tiki was a two-foot-long bearded dragon with beady, red-rimmed eyes. The first time Andy introduced me to Tiki, the thing puffed out its spiny neck and opened its jaw so wide I was sure it would attack, if given half a chance.

I felt goose bumps popping out on my arms as my eyes darted around the floor.

Would it be rude to stand on a chair?

As a homeschooling mother of four, Jess put up with a menagerie of animals in her home—both warm and cold blooded. Every once in a while, my Hannah would report gleefully that another member of the "zoo" next door had escaped. Then she'd beg to "pluueeeeese" spend the night with Claire to help find it—because "snakes are nocturnal, you know."

Could Hannah have been switched at birth?

"Jess!" Marina pounds on the basement wall to get our attention. "You've got a big, hairy-lookin' lizard crouched in your furnace flickin' his tongue at me. And a guy on your basement floor who needs some smelling salts."

"Tiki!" Andy charged down the stairs.

I decided to abandon all sense of propriety and casually climbed on a kitchen chair.

●

*Y*es, Tiki's rescue definitely took the prize as the most memorable FAC. But yesterday was a close second.

I about fell out of my chair when perfectly groomed and mannered Mary Alice revealed that her parents were flower children. It's too much to fathom. From the way she's described her *Leave It to Beaver* childhood, I'd thought of her mother as a pillar of the Junior League—not the Green Party.

But what really breaks my heart is that M.A. felt she had to make up a charmed childhood to cope with the pain. Consequently, I didn't have the heart to ask her all the questions boiling inside me. And I had lots of questions.

So dear, sweet John had become the target for all my speculation as soon as I'd been able to corner him last night. Unfortunately, he'd started to get that glazed look well before I was talked out. This morning I hope he'll have more stamina. Especially since I've made his favorite breakfast.

But as I carry the tray up the stairs, I can't help feeling a few twinges of guilt. Not just because I know John isn't as interested as I am in discussing these new revelations about Mary Alice's past. From experience and what my friends tell me, I know that most husbands aren't the best choice for conversations that require no solutions—merely uninterrupted listening. Once they have the facts, they're satisfied. No need to "talk everything to death."

But I need to *dish*. Which leads to the second source of my unease.

Is "dishing" considered gossip when it's with your husband? I know gossip is wrong. After all, I've studied the book of Proverbs and all those verses warning about the "tongue." For a while I even wrote Proverbs 18:21 on a sticky note and posted it by the phone. "Words kill, words give life; they're either poison or fruit—you choose." That verse sure shot down a lot of juicy conversations.

I know it would be gossiping to call up a friend outside of FAC to talk about Mary Alice's formerly secret storage unit. I'd never think of doing that. Well . . . it might cross my mind if I were desperate. But I wouldn't actually make the call.

It's probably also crossing the line to call another woman from my Bible study to pray about the situation when—if I'm honest with myself—what I really want to do is dish. I'd even feel a little funny calling one of my FAC friends just to dish. Unless I could think of some other reason to call, of course, and last night's topic of conversation just happened to come up. But if I have to think of an excuse to call, then my real intention is to dish anyway. So that nullifies the whole thing.

If only I had the patience to wait until FAC gets together this afternoon to help Mary Alice sort through the stuff in her storage unit. We'll talk plenty then. But that's five hours away. If I don't do something soon, I'll start in on comfort food. And my jeans are already too tight.

So John wins—and breakfast in bed is his prize for listening to me. After all, didn't God bind us together as one when we got married? For times like these? To keep me from gossiping?

I shove aside my guilt and push open the door to our bedroom with my hip.

*

*J*ohn's eyes light up at the sight of the tray laden with his favorite breakfast—Blueberry Pancakes and Cinnamon-Sugared Bacon. As I set up the bamboo tray on the bed, I'm counting on the food perking him up enough to at least pretend to listen.

"John, can you believe Mary Alice has been keeping this secret about her father in all these years?" I hand him a long-stemmed glass of Sparkling Juice with a fresh strawberry on the rim.

"Ummm," he says, taking a sip, "didn't we talk about this last night?"

"Just for a minute—right before bed. You haven't heard the whole story."

"I think we talked longer than—"

"Did I tell you Mary Alice's dad left before her first birthday? That breaks my heart."

"Yes. You mentioned it last night."

"John, can you imagine abandoning me and the kids to go live on some commune?"

He looks up from his plate, brown eyes wide. "Of course not, I would never—"

"And she says her father spent most of his life living in a van. A *van*. Can you believe it?"

He smirks. "Not when I think of the shape of our minivan after only a week of carpool. Liz, I wish you'd keep the kids from eating in—"

I shake my finger at him. "No fair trying to change the subject. I made you breakfast in bed. You owe me a friendly ear."

John takes a forkful of pancakes and leans back on the pillows propping up his back. His sandy hair is sticking up in all the wrong places. "These *are* good."

How can a man look so adorable with bed head?

I smile. "Thank you. Anyway, as I was saying, Mary Alice says she has no idea what's in that storage unit." I snatch a slice of bacon from his plate and bite into it. "I mean, she had the whole kit-and-caboodle delivered six months ago and hasn't even taken a peek."

"You mentioned that last night." He grins.

"But do you think it's true? I mean, how could anyone *not* look? Especially after all this time?" I take another nibble of bacon.

John rolls his neck from side to side, as if trying to work out a crick. "Well, if she said she hasn't looked, then—"

"Impossible," I blurt out. "Could you keep from opening a package for six months?"

"I guess if I had a good reason to—"

"You could not! I know you, John. There's no way you could sit on a package for six months."

"I said if I had a good reason not to open—"

"You're fooling yourself. No one has that much self-control. You may think you do, but I *know* you. And trust me, you don't."

"Well, obviously, Mary Alice has that kind of control because—"

Why do men always have to be so logical?

"You have a point there," I reluctantly admit. "Control is her middle name. Hmmm . . ." I nab another piece of bacon off his plate.

As I savor the crispy morsel, it occurs to me how much I love bacon. I rue the day that South Beach doctor took all the fun out of low-carb dieting. Like anyone is truly happy living on salmon and turkey breast.

This gives me an idea for my column, which happens to be due in two days. I kiss John on the forehead—satisfactorily talked out for now. *Is that relief I see in his eyes?*

I want to get my ideas on paper before I forget them.

●

*A*fter bribing Josh to chauffeur Hannah to dance class, I sit down at my computer to write my column for the Omaha World-Herald.

This time last year I dreaded the weekly commitment. I was always afraid someone would expose me for the not-so-perfect homemaker I really am. I secretly feared the existence of a "truth in media" squad that would show up on a lazy Saturday morning to do a surprise inspection of my closets. Or that a team of pompous French chefs would put my culinary skills to the test by forcing me to prepare a five-course gourmet meal from ingredients I had on hand—all the while clucking their disapproval and making surreptitious notes. I even feared my own mother would un-knowingly expose my ineptitude in the laundry room to a shady tabloid reporter, resulting in my picture splashed on the cover with the headline "Lifestyle Columnist Wreaks Havoc with Oxybooster!"

However, since coming clean with my fans last fall and admitting I don't have all the answers to their domestic dilemmas, I've come to relish my time at the keyboard. This morning the words are flowing so fast that my fingers have trouble keeping up.

Loving Life!

By Elizabeth Harris

As I savored a piece of bacon (yes, bacon!) this morning, it occurred to me how "uncool" it is these days to admit eating this smoked delight from a pig's underbelly. In fact, it wasn't until the advent of the protein diet that I even dared to venture to the "bacon" section of the supermarket—except during the Christmas season when everyone does away with healthy eating. After all, we need something to resolve not to do on New Year's. Just hearing about a new diet with bacon on the "free food" list put me in Hog Heaven. Literally.

Now that the healthcare industry has weighed in, the only politically correct proteins are low-fat. Or those with "good" fat like olive oil, salmon, or soy nuts. I have to shield my eyes in the checkout line to avoid reading the magazine covers. I'm afraid I'll see a headline announcing new research proving that women over forty who wear elastic waists are at risk for some horrendous disease that can only be cured by a complete—and permanent—fast from chocolate.

So today, my dear readers, I encourage you to seize the day! You never know what you'll need to give up for the sake of moderation. Here are a few ideas to help you get started.

1. Drink good coffee. Life is too short to waste it on Robusta beans. Find a mellow French Roast of good-quality Arabica beans and enjoy it. Even if you don't have a cents-off coupon.

2. Take a brisk walk when you get up in the morning. Then come home and enjoy a great breakfast. Better yet, take a walk with a friend to a nearby coffee shop. You won't feel nearly as guilty savoring a mocha latté.

3. Make your bed. It only takes a minute, and there's nothing better at the end of a long day than crawling between smooth sheets.

4. Take a bath—and not just to get clean. Use a scented bubble bath, light candles, play soft music. Set up a tray of chocolate-covered strawberries on the side of the tub. Pretend you are in a luxury suite with a staff outside the door waiting to attend to your every need. But, of course, you are much too polite to ask.

5. Buy a backscratcher—and keep it handy. The best $1.99 I ever spent was for a wooden stick with one end carved to resemble a little claw. I realize what a stroke of genius this purchase is every time I pull it out of my

bedside table to satisfy an itch. Pedestrian,
but so true.

6. Finally, while some suggest taking time to
   smell the roses, I disagree. Lilacs smell
   much sweeter. Always take time to smell a
   lilac bush—the flowers don't last long.

So *carpe diem*, dear reader! This week join me in LOVING
LIFE—and savoring bacon!

As I press *Send*, zipping the column through cyberspace to my editor,
I realize the key to viewing writing with relish instead of as a chore is being passionate about your subject.

Even if it is bacon.

●

The FAC gang agreed last night to meet at Jessie's house and drive out
to Storage Unlimited in her Suburban. Since Jess has four kids, she can
drive a monster SUV without getting accosted by anxious environmental
activists wielding pamphlets about global warming. After all, the SUV is
more energy efficient than a school bus.

While I cut across my lawn to her house, an unexpected melancholy
begins to edge out my excitement. I remember the parting conversation
with Mary Alice and Lucy as we huddled on my front porch yesterday
after the others had headed home . . .

●

I don't know if I can handle going through that storage unit." Mary
Alice pulled her sweater close around her. "I know it's best to get it over
with. But I'm starting to lose my nerve."

Lucy gave her a one-armed hug. "Oh, sweetie, I know. But waiting won't make it any easier." She smiled gently. "And trying to stuff the pain behind busyness won't keep it down forever."

Mary Alice turned to gaze at the sunset and rubbed her arms as if trying to chase away a chill. "On good days, when I was a little girl, I could think of him as a kind of mythic hero. Not willing to compromise his passion for the environment and fight against what he considered the hypocrisy of the government. At least he stood for something. Which was more than I could say for myself.

"But on bad days—when I felt like an outcast because I didn't have a father around like the other kids—I just considered him a bum. He abandoned my mother and me. What kind of a husband and father is that? I could never do that to one of my children."

As Mary Alice spoke, I thought of my own dad. When I was a child, he was the center of our family. A rock I could always depend on. And today he is still that rock. My heart ached for my friend.

"I've lied all my life about my father until the lies seem true, even to me," Mary Alice added, tears threatening to spill over her lashes. "But opening that storage unit is going to make me face the truth. Whatever is in there is what he chose over me. And I can barely stand the thought of looking at it.

"I know it's going to be a bunch of worthless junk," she said with a catch in her voice. "So what does that say about me?"

CHAPTER FIVE

MARY ALICE'S RECIPE FOR A
SWEET-SMELLING HOME

1. Combine 1 teaspoon vinegar, 1 tablespoon baking soda, and 2 cups water in a spray bottle. When the mixture stops foaming, spray into the air to neutralize stubborn odors.

2. Soak 3 cotton balls in vanilla. Place in an uncovered dish to freshen the air.

3. Freshen carpets by mixing 3 parts baking soda, 1 part scented talcum powder, and 1 part cornstarch. Sprinkle on carpets. Let sit for at least 20 minutes. Vacuum thoroughly.

SPICY AIR FRESHENER

This great homemade air freshener has a fresh, clean scent.

2 tablespoons dried sage

4 tablespoons bay leaves

8 ounces witch hazel

Instructions

1. Crumble sage and bay leaves in a glass container. Add witch hazel.
2. Cover tightly and store in a dark closet for 3 days.
3. Strain liquid into an atomizer. Spray to freshen air.

So where's Marina?" Jess and I are standing next to her Suburban while Kelly maneuvers into the back row of seats. At five foot two and just a hair over 105 pounds, we figure sitting in the back is the least Kelly can do to assuage our envy over her figure.

Jess catches up her long hair with one hand and pulls it to one side. "Marina's twins had a soccer game this morning. She called to tell me she'll meet us at Storage Unlimited. And she's bringing lunch."

I climb into the vehicle and slide across the middle seat to sit next to Lucy. "Marina's in the kitchen again? I'm glad I ate early."

Jess laughs as she climbs behind the wheel. "She says she made something special for us."

"Now I'm really nervous. My kitchen still smells like those Greaseballs of hers. Or should I call them 'fireballs'?"

Mary Alice, who is sitting shotgun next to Jess, glances over her shoulder into the back seat. "Didn't you get my e-mail, Liz? The recipe for odor neutralizer works wonders."

Mary Alice is the only woman I know who, in the midst of such emotional turmoil, would have the presence of mind to forward me a list of homemade air fresheners. Fortunately, I catch myself before a snarky comment escapes my lips. Considering the circumstances, I better be nice.

●

It amazes me how some women are just like men when it comes to asking for directions. It's like finding a place without a map is a badge of honor. I once asked John what the attraction was to driving around without knowing where you're going.

He quoted *The Lord of the Rings*. "Tolkien says, 'Not all who are searching are lost.'"

I've got to keep him away from the movies.

Most women would much rather ask for directions or get a map than drive around lost. But not Kelly.

"What's the number on your key again, M.A.?" she shouts from the seat behind me.

We've been circling the maze of storage buildings for ten minutes in search of Mary Alice's unit. We could have stopped at the manager's office for a map. But no. Kelly, who claims to have a natural sense of direction, convinced us it was a waste of time.

"The key says G-12-16. But maybe I'm reading it wrong." Mary Alice hands me the key. "What do you think, Liz?"

I squint at the tiny engraved numbers, straining without my reading glasses. "That's what it looks like to me."

Kelly reaches across the backseat. "Here, let me look at it."

"I'm sorry I'm not more help," says Mary Alice in a tiny voice. "I've only been out here a couple of times to pay the rent. And then only to the manager's office."

I'm still having trouble believing that M.A. has been renting this unit for the last six months and hasn't taken even a tiny peek. Talk about a study in self-control. If only she could bottle it. Then maybe I'd have the willpower to stay on my diet and the hope of seeing a size 8 again.

"Do you think the unit could be at another location, M.A.?" says Lucy. "I haven't seen any buildings with a G on them. The sequence stops at D."

"This is why they make maps," I mumble under my breath.

Kelly either didn't hear me or chose to ignore my comment. "Jess, circle the perimeter one more time. We must have missed it."

"Once more—then I'm heading to the office for a map."

Where does Jess get her patience? I feel like I'm on an endless trek through a jungle of corrugated steel with the tiny leader of the safari cracking the whip from the back seat. If I were driving, I would have confiscated her whip a long time ago.

"What about that building over there?" I point to a fenced parking lot full of RVs and boats with a low building of what looks to be overhead garage doors at the far end.

"That's where Michael stores our boat." Jess jerks the wheel to make a sharp left. "Might as well check it out."

"No, Jess, that couldn't be my unit. Those all look like garages."

"If you've never been there, how do you know?" asks Jess.

"Good point," I offer.

"My dad was basically homeless. He couldn't have accumulated that much stuff."

"You never know, M.A.," teases Jess. "Maybe your talent for organization and storage solutions is genetic."

Kelly pats my shoulder. "Now maybe you have an excuse for that hall closet, Liz."

●

*J*ess is right. We find Unit G-12-16 in the building behind the RVs, where all the units measure ten-by-twenty feet—the size of a single-car garage.

To say Mary Alice is surprised is putting it mildly. "I guess I didn't look very closely at the rental agreement. I certainly didn't think my space was this large. What could he have in here? You guys can back out if you want. We'll be here all afternoon."

Maybe on Mary Alice's "no dawdling" timetable. But today she'll have to live by FAC time. I seriously doubt we'll get done this afternoon. The thought of sorting through all the stuff hibernating behind the door is both exciting and overwhelming.

After wrangling the padlock open, Kelly turns around, shielding her eyes from the afternoon sun. We are lined up like a row of outlaws facing the overhead garage door—our shadows forming a stark tableau before us.

"Ready to see what's in here?" she asks.

Mary Alice looks at the ground. "I guess."

Lucy steps forward to grab one of the handles near the bottom of the metal door. "Let me give you a hand."

"Thanks, Luce. Okay, here goes."

The two women bend and lift the heavy door. It rolls open with a groan—steel rollers creaking along the tracks. The scraping of metal upon metal doesn't shock me as much as the brilliant flash of sunlight reflected by the huge object behind the door.

I raise my hand to protect my eyes.

Wow.

chapter SIX

TURKISH COFFEE

3/4 cup water

1 tablespoon sugar

1 tablespoon very finely ground coffee (pulverized)

1 cardamom pod

Instructions

1. Combine water and sugar in an ibrik* or small saucepan. Bring to a boil.
2. Remove from heat and add coffee and cardamom. Stir well and return to heat.
3. When coffee foams up, remove from heat and let grounds settle. Repeat 3 times. Remove cardamom pod.
4. Pour into espresso or demitasse cups. Let grounds settle before drinking.

Makes 2 espresso-sized cups.

* An ibrik is a small, long-handled pot. It is sometimes referred to as a cezves. The top of the pot is smaller than the bottom, which is important for the proper brewing of Turkish coffee. The shape allows the coffee to form a cap on top and the boiling water to bubble up over the grounds.

CHIP CHAT

20 thick-cut potato chips (like Kettle chips)

1 cup plain yogurt

1/2 teaspoon salt

Additional spices to taste: red chili powder, ground cumin, jeera (black cumin seeds), chopped cilantro

Instructions

1. Arrange chips on a serving plate.
2. Stir salt into yogurt and spread on chips.
3. Sprinkle chili powder, ground cumin, jeera, and cilantro.
4. Serve immediately.

PATCHOULI PERFUME OIL

3 drops patchouli

3 drops sandalwood

1 ounce almond oil

Instructions

1. Mix together in a small glass container.
2. Use to scent skin or bath.

September, 1966

LOS ANGELES—*The Dick Van Dyke Show* swept the 12th Annual Emmy Awards, taking home the prize for Outstanding Comedy Series, Outstanding Performance by a Comedic Actor in a Leading Role (Dick Van Dyke), Outstanding Performance by a Comedic Actress in a Leading Role (Mary Tyler Moore) and Outstanding Writing Achievement in Comedy (Bill Persky and Sam Denoff). Don Knotts received the award for Best Supporting Actor for his work on *The Andy Griffith Show* as did Alice Pearce for Best Supporting Actress on *Bewitched*.

●

Denny O'Brien stood back to inspect his work. He had saved for two summers to buy Camille—a 1963 Volkswagen minibus. Her two-tone look, split windscreen, and V-shaped front made her a classic. Now, as he put finishing touches on the psychedelic design adorning the exterior, the van was finally starting to look like his.

He'd already spent a couple hundred bucks wrapping the interior with a rust-colored shag carpet. His little sister had made some groovy curtains from sheets she'd tie-dyed. And he'd even installed one of those new FM converters under the dash for his radio.

Last week he'd paid a buddy to paint the two-tone exterior a Day-Glo orange and electric purple. This served as the backdrop for the psychedelic swirls winding their way along the hood and sides of the vehicle. The peace sign replacing the VW logo between the headlights left no question about Denny's political views.

"If I could just get the letters right," he mumbled as he eyed the van parked in front of his apartment on Hitt Street near the University of Missouri–Columbia campus.

"Maybe you need a little soul and inspiration." A familiar female voice mimicked the lyrics from the Righteous Brothers' latest hit. A pair of arms slipped around his waist and pulled him close.

He sighed, leaning back into the embrace before slowly turning to face the petite young woman in fringed, bell-bottomed blue jeans and sandals.

"Hey, babe. You finished with class already?"

"Finally. Tabor made us spend the entire lab identifying twigs. After today, I'm not sure horticulture is really my bag."

Denny tucked a loose strand of the girl's long, straight blond hair behind her ear and breathed in the musky fragrance of the Patchouli Oil she'd begun to wear lately. "Poor Ali. Maybe you need to mellow out for a while."

"I *do* need something to take my mind off school. You need some help with those letters?"

"If you're offering . . ." Denny pushed his shaggy brown hair out of his eyes. He watched as Ali circled the van, examining the words he had sketched out on the body in pencil. Ali was pretty creative. She lettered all the signs for the Chez—the coffeehouse where she worked part-time—and had made a name for herself with her Turkish Coffee and a spicy Indian snack called Chip Chat.

"Okay. I see your problem." Ali pointed to the outline of *PEACE* that Denny had sketched in block letters. "You're using too many angles."

Denny walked to her side to take a closer look. "Babe, I think you've been sniffing some strange plants in Tabor's class. Most of the letters of the alphabet have angles. Maybe you should take a couple of engineering classes with me."

"You're such a chauvinist pig, O'Brien!" Ali, green eyes flashing, nudged him playfully with her elbow. "Let's see . . . how can I explain this so someone who spends most of his day with a slide rule will understand?"

Denny smirked. "Very funny."

"Seriously, Den, try to imagine that the letters are expanding into the universe. Dig?" Ali took the pencil from Denny and began to sketch the word *LOVE* in large loopy letters. "See? You want the letters to all connect."

Denny moved behind her, his beard brushing her neck, as he reached around so Ali could guide his hand. "Here—let me follow your strokes. Maybe I'll pick up some of your creative vibe."

She turned around to face him, slipping her arms around his neck. Her soft breath tickled his chin. "I'm starting to lose interest in Camille."

Now Denny remembered why he had chased this girl for four years at their small-town high school in Rock Port, Missouri. And spent the summer convincing her to transfer from Kansas State to Mizzou after her freshman year. He was also pretty close to talking this small-town girl into taking Camille on a road trip after Christmas break to San Francisco for what they were calling "The Gathering of the Tribes." This was the beginning of something big—and Denny wasn't about to miss it.

"Ali, you are definitely not in Kansas anymore."

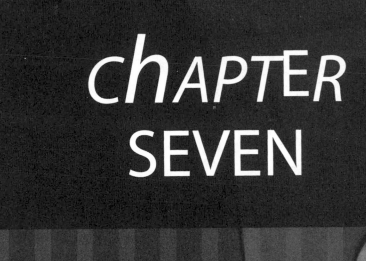

chapter SEVEN

MARINA'S ITALIAN BEEF POOR BOYS

3 cloves garlic, minced

1 teaspoon salt

1/4 teaspoon freshly ground pepper

1 beef bottom round roast (approximately 4 pounds)

1 large jar roasted sweet red peppers (or more if you really like
   peppers)

1 tablespoon instant beef bouillon granules

1 teaspoon dried Italian seasoning

1/2 teaspoon dried oregano

1/2 teaspoon crushed red pepper

16 crusty Italian rolls, split

Instructions

1. Mix together garlic, salt, and pepper. Rub over roast.

2. Place meat on rack in roasting pan. Insert meat
   thermometer into thickest part of roast.

3. Roast at 300 degrees until meat thermometer registers 135
   degrees. This should take about 1–1 1/2 hours for a 4 pound
   roast.

4. Remove roast, cover, and refrigerate.

5. Pour drippings into a measuring cup. Skim off fat, and
   reserve.

6. While beef chills, place red peppers facedown in broiler pan.
   Broil 10–15 minutes or until skins blister. Put hot peppers in
   a closed paper bag for 10–20 minutes to make skins easier
   to remove. Cut peppers into 1-inch strips.

7. Add water to drippings to equal 5 cups and pour into a Dutch oven. Add bouillon granules, Italian seasoning, oregano, and red pepper. Bring to a boil and simmer 10 minutes.
8. Carve roast across the grain into very thin slices. A meat slicer works best—or ask your butcher to slice it for you. Add beef and peppers to liquid. Cover and heat just until hot throughout.
9. Serve beef on crusty Italian rolls, topped with roasted red peppers and gravy.

MOSTACCIOLI SALAD

1 pound mostaccioli pasta

3 tablespoons olive oil

1/2 cup sugar

1/2 cup red wine vinegar

1 teaspoon salt

1/2 teaspoon pepper

1 teaspoon Accent seasoning

2 teaspoons crushed garlic

2 teaspoons prepared mustard

1 medium red onion, thinly sliced

1 medium cucumber, diced

1 sweet bell pepper, thinly sliced

1 tablespoon fresh parsley, chopped

Instructions

1. Cook noodles al dente. Drain and toss with olive oil.
2. Mix sugar, vinegar, salt, pepper, Accent, garlic, and mustard. Add to pasta with vegetables. Toss to coat.
3. Refrigerate. This is best if made 1 or 2 days ahead.
4. Just before serving, sprinkle with fresh parsley.

Serves 8.

CANNOLI

2 cups ricotta cheese

1 cup powdered sugar

2 teaspoons fresh grated orange peel

1/2 cup mascarpone cheese*

1/4 teaspoon vanilla extract

1/3 cup minced crystallized ginger

1/3 cup minced dried cherries

2 ounces semisweet chocolate, chopped

12 cannoli shells*

Chopped pistachios

Additional powdered sugar

Instructions

1. Blend ricotta, powdered sugar, orange peel, mascarpone, and vanilla in food processor until smooth.
2. Add ginger and cherries and process until well incorporated.
3. Pulse to mix in chocolate just until blended.
4. Transfer filling to a pastry bag without a tip. Or you can use a self-sealing bag with one bottom corner snipped off. Pipe filling into shells.
5. Sprinkle ends with pistachios.
6. Chill at least 2 hours and up to 6 hours.
7. Sift powdered sugar over cannoli just before serving.

Makes 1 dozen.

* These items are now available at many supermarkets but can almost always be found at Italian specialty markets.

I guess now we know why you needed a garage."

I'm generally the one who can be counted on to state the obvious. And I always end up taking a lot of grief for it. But this time, as we stare at the old VW minibus that has hulked in Mary Alice's storage unit for the last six months, my friends seem too stunned to notice.

Vintage is much too nice a word for this vehicle, which appears to be held together by fragile tendrils of rust and a few strategically placed strips of duct tape. All four tires are flat so that the van appears to be huddled on the cement floor like a sleeping cat.

Lucy walks forward, gingerly running her index finger along the weather-pitted front bumper. "I'm not sure what I was expecting, but it definitely wasn't this."

Kelly bends down to peer under the chassis. "It must have cost a fortune to get this here. It's obvious no one drove it."

"My dad's friend had it shipped, so . . ."

Jess grabs Mary Alice's elbow as her knees begin to buckle.

●

*I'*m sorry. I can't go through with this." Mary Alice is sitting in Jess's Suburban, eyes closed, head resting back against the seat. "I thought I could, but I can't."

"Yes, you can. And you will."

For once, I am grateful for Kelly's take-charge attitude. She has spent the last ten minutes calming Mary Alice down while the rest of us milled around without a clue how to help. Even Jess seems at a loss. Other than helping to get Mary Alice to the car, Jess has been uncharacteristically silent.

"Hey *chicas*!" Never one to make a quiet entrance, Marina pulls up next to the Suburban. "I didn't think I'd ever find you. Whaddya doin' all the way back here?"

I walk over to Marina's big, blue convertible. "M.A.'s storage unit is around the corner. We got it open but ran into a little snafu. By the way, isn't it a little chilly to have the top down?"

"I didn't want my Italian beef stinking up the car."

I grimace. "Now I feel better about what you brought for lunch."

"Trust me, Lizzie, you'll love it. It's my mom's recipe. I even brought you a cannoli."

My eyes brighten. I've tasted Marina's cannolis. "Just one cannoli?"

Marina laughs. "Let me park this boat; then I'll get you slackers back to work."

●

I have to hand it to Kelly. She may be brusque at times, but she knew just what to do to get Mary Alice moving. Shortly after Marina arrived, Kelly appointed Lucy and Mary Alice to set up our tailgate lunch in the rear of Jess's SUV. Back in her comfort zone of domesticity, M.A. has lost the distraught look that I hadn't seen since I was a crime reporter fresh out of journalism school . . . on the faces at the scene of a fire as the victims watched their worldly possessions transformed into a pile of ash.

"So this is it? No boxes?" Marina is in the garage, circling the minibus like a crime scene. "Where's the rest of his stuff?"

"Maybe inside the van?" Jess uses the sleeve of her sweatshirt to wipe a spot clean on the dusty rear window.

"There's no use standing around. Let's open her up." Kelly tugs open the side passenger door.

"Shouldn't we make sure it's okay with Mary Alice before we go rooting through her dad's things?" I ask.

Marina snorts. Kelly sighs and climbs in the front seat. And Jess puts her arm around my shoulders and gives me a reassuring squeeze. "That's why we're here, sweetie."

"I know, but . . ."

Marina glares at me over her shoulder. "Lizzie, sometimes you gotta pull the chestnuts outta the fire. That's what friends are for." She yanks open the door on the driver's side of the van.

I look at Jess. "What's that supposed to mean?"

"Who knows? But I'm not about to ask. Let's give them a hand."

●

*U*nlike the chaotic paint design on the exterior of the van, the interior is a model of organization and utility.

"Look at this," says Marina as I open the door on the passenger side, exposing a pass-through with facing bench seats and a rustic wood table in-between. "You can flip the table to make a bed."

"And look at this." I lift the corner of a faded bedspread that's draped over the seat. A row of cabinets are built beneath. "There's more storage here than I had in my first kitchen."

Marina nods approvingly. "Guy must have been pretty handy to trick out the interior like this. Can't wait to see the green-eyed monster rear his head when Jeff gets a load of this baby."

"So are you seeing Jeff tonight?" I am doing my best to sound casual. I hate to be so obvious about my interest in Marina's love life, but we were all there to see the sparks fly when she met Jeff during the renovation of Lucy's home. And we've had a front-row seat ever since for the bonfire that's been building. Marina's birthday is this summer, and I'd be surprised if she doesn't get a ring.

Before Marina can answer my question about her plans for the evening, Jess calls from the rear of the van. "Could someone give me a hand here? I've found some things we might want to go through together."

"What is it, Jess?" Mary Alice's voice makes me jump, almost toppling the stack of shoeboxes I've dragged from a cupboard under the seat.

"M.A., you scared me to death!" I rise from my squatting position.

"I just came to tell you that lunch is set up whenever you're ready for it. What'd you find, Jess?"

"It looks like a box of old papers. I thought there might be something important in there. We can sort through it later." Jess puts the box down on the cement floor.

"No need. It's probably just trash." Mary Alice opens the flap of the box and pulls out the cream-colored flyer on top of the stack.

chapter EIGHT

COFFEE CAN BREAD

2 1/2 cups warm water (not over 85 degrees)

1 package yeast

1 tablespoon flour

1 tablespoon sugar, honey, or molasses

4 cups whole-wheat flour

2 teaspoons salt

1/2 cup powdered milk

Instructions

1. Combine water, yeast, 1 tablespoon flour, and 1 tablespoon sugar (or other sweetener) in small bowl. Allow mixture to stand until bubbly.

2. In a large bowl, sift together flour, salt, and powdered milk.

3. Add liquid mixture to dry ingredients. Combine but do not knead. Cover bowl with a damp towel. Let dough stand in a warm place for approximately 2 hours.

   Tip: To create a warm place, heat oven to lowest temperature—usually 150 degrees. Turn off. Place bowl in oven and leave door cracked open.

4. When dough has doubled, turn out on floured surface and knead 10–15 minutes. Keep just enough flour on the board and hands to prevent sticking. Use the heels of your hands to push out, fold over, and push out again until dough begins to develop elasticity. You will know the dough is right when it feels like it is pushing back.

5. Divide dough in half and shape into 2 balls. Place each in a well-greased 1-pound coffee can. Let rise about 45 minutes until it just reaches top of can. Bake in a preheated 350-degree oven approximately 55 minutes.

January 14, 1967

SAN FRANCISCO—A massive crowd of mostly students and antiwar protesters began to converge on Golden Gate Park earlier today for what organizers are calling a "Human Be-In." Many leaders of the counterculture movement are expected to be in attendance, including Dr. Timothy Leary, Allen Ginsberg, Gary Snyder, and Jerry Rubin. Participants have been asked to bring food to share, flowers, beads, costumes, feathers, bells, cymbals, and flags. Thus far, no incidents of violence have been reported among the crowd some estimate to be near 20,000.

●

"How come your old lady didn't come out with you, Denny?"

The two bearded young men sat on a curb in the rundown Haight-Ashbury district of San Francisco, sharing a loaf of bread provided by the Diggers Free Bakery. It seemed to Denny that everything was free in California. Free food, free love, and freedom from responsibility.

The childhood friends had met in the city early that morning. Denny had driven cross-country from Missouri in just two days, taking short naps in the back of Camille when he couldn't keep his eyes open any longer. Steve had hitch-hiked from nearby Santa Cruz, where he attended the University of California.

Denny looked up from the cream-colored handbill with "The Gathering of the Tribes for a Human Be-In" printed across the top in an artistic script.

"Huh? What'd you say, Steve?"

The young man tossed his long hair away from his face, then pulled a piece of wheat bread from the coffee can between his legs and crammed it in his mouth. "Where's your head at, man?" he asked between bites. "I was just wondering why Ali didn't make the road trip with you."

Denny folded the flyer and shoved it into his pocket. "She hasn't been feeling so good since she found out she was pregnant."

"That's a drag. About her being sick," he quickly countered. "Not the kid."

"Yeah, I knew what you meant, bro." Denny was still getting used to the idea of Ali being pregnant himself. They hadn't planned on a baby this soon but . . .

Steve interrupted his thoughts. "I have to tell you, man, you are blowin' me away here. First you give in to The System and get married. Now Ali's knocked up. Next you'll be working for The Man and building one of those tract houses in the suburbs."

"Not Ali and me, man. We're thinking about joining a collective with some people that have gone back to the land. Ali wants to grow our own food. Keep things pure for the baby."

"Righteous." Steve nodded and tore another chunk of bread off with his teeth.

A girl with vacant eyes, wearing an orange and yellow Indian print dress and a crown of dandelions in her tangled hair, squatted in front of Denny. She placed a grimy hand on his cheek and a wilted flower in his shirt pocket.

"Uh, thanks," he replied.

Flashing a weak smile, the girl rose on shaky legs and snaked away in a swirl of color.

Steve laughed as he watched her stumble down the street. "Yeah. The flower children are ripe for the picking out here on the coast. Just follow the incense . . . all the way to heaven."

Denny felt a familiar stirring. "I wish I could have talked Ali into coming with me. But she's been so uptight lately. Maybe she'll loosen up when we move to the country."

"What are you gonna do about college while you and Ali are getting back to nature? Before you know it, Uncle Sam will be calling your number to good old Viet-NAM."

"I'm already 4-F, buddy. Hurt my knee playing football. If The Man says I'm unfit for service, who am I to argue?"

Steve laughed. "Far-out. Hey, we better get over to Golden Gate Park. We don't want to miss the party."

●

The Gathering of the Tribes." Mary Alice grunts as she reads the old handbill. "Sounds a little arrogant to me."

Jessie and I peer at the heavily creased piece of paper over Mary Alice's shoulder.

"This looks like an original," Jess says. "Can I see it?"

"A Human Be-In?" Mary Alice laughs derisively and hands the paper to Jess. "It's original all right."

Jessie sits cross-legged on the cement floor and examines the flyer. It pictures an Eastern holy man with a triangle superimposed over a third eye in the middle of his forehead.

"I remember my older brother arguing with my parents about this when he was home from Berkeley for Christmas break." Jessie swoops her long hair to one side. "My dad found the flyer in his bag and forbid him to go to 'some hippie love-in.'

"Mark was really upset—so I told him I'd be in his tribe." Jess smiles at the memory.

I sink down next to her on the floor as she begins to rummage through the box. "I always knew down deep you were a flower child."

Marina pops her head out from inside the van. "Good detective work, Lizzie. What gave it away—the Birkenstocks or her library of organic gardening books?"

I decide to ignore Marina. I, for one, know how to "go with the flow." Groove with the vibe. Dance with the—

"Look at this." Jessie plucks a faded but colorful copy of a newspaper from the box. "It's an old copy of the *San Francisco Oracle*."

Mary Alice glances over her shoulder. "Looks like some old hippie newspaper. The design is enough to cause hallucinations."

I look up to see Lucy standing in the doorway of the storage unit holding a box full of sandwiches. "Since you didn't come out to lunch, I thought I'd bring it to you. I was getting lonely out there. Not to mention hungry."

Mary Alice glances around the cramped storage unit. "Well, we can't eat in here."

"Oh yes we can." Marina hits the side of the van with her fist. "This baby has a built-in table. And if I get tired after lunch, I'll just flip it over and take a nap."

Mary Alice wrinkles her nose. "You can't be serious. That old van has to be filthy inside."

I push myself up from the floor. "Maybe a little dated. But it's not bad at all."

Marina steps down from the van and takes the box of food from Lucy. "Looks like you got your neatnik genes from your dad, M.A."

"No, we can't possibly . . ." Mary Alice looks around anxiously.

Jess stands up. "Come on, M.A. It's better than eating outside. At least we won't have to sit on the asphalt."

"All that pollen is playing havoc with my allergies anyway," adds Kelly.

Mary Alice persists. "It has to be stuffy in there. And what about the dust?"

"This beauty opens up on both sides. There's enough of a cross breeze to even chase one of Lizzie's hot flashes away." Marina slaps me on the back.

"Ha. Ha," I say as heat begins to creep up my neck.

●

*T*his is so strange sitting in here." Mary Alice passes the box of Marina's Italian Beef Poor Boys across the table to Jess and me. She is sitting on the bench seat with Kelly and Lucy. Marina is perched on a box at the end of the table.

Lucy scoops a dainty spoonful of Mostaccioli Salad from a plastic container. "You have to admit it's cozy."

"And well organized." Kelly takes the salad container from Lucy. "The storage is ingenious."

Jess runs her hand over one of the knotty-pine cabinets. "Whoever made these cabinets was quite a craftsman."

"I think my dad used to like to work with wood. My mom still has a box of animals he carved for me when I was a baby."

"That's so sweet," I say. "I bet—"

Kelly gives me a stern look and changes the subject. "Jess, you were going to tell us about this Gathering of the Tribes."

Kelly's on a mission, and I assume she's concerned discussion of M.A.'s dad is going to set off another blast of emotions. I decide to bite my tongue.

"I was still in grammar school," says Jess, "so I don't remember much firsthand. But from what I've read, The Gathering is considered by many people to be the defining event of the counterculture movement. It's where Timothy Leary told kids to 'turn on, tune in, and drop out.'"

"I bet he was the darling of parents everywhere," Lucy says grimly.

Kelly nods. "Wasn't he also the guy who said don't trust anyone over thirty?"

"I don't know if he's the one who said it, but I thought it was a pretty good idea," says Marina. "At least until I hit forty."

I look up from my plate. "You mean until you hit thirty, right?"

"No. I meant forty." Marina raises her eyebrows. "You know I've never looked my age."

A collective groan fills the small space, causing even Mary Alice to smile.

I take a bite of my sandwich. It is really good. Maybe there's hope for Marina's cooking after all.

"So Jess, how do you know so much about the counterculture?" asks Kelly.

"I've always been interested in the idealism of the sixties."

Lucy smiles. "You? Idealistic? I never would have believed it."

Jess returns her smile. "There was a lot of good that came from the sixties. Unfortunately, a lot of it was lost as a result of—"

"A purple haze?" blurts out Marina.

Now I'm the one to deliver a swift kick under the table. This time to Marina. The last thing Mary Alice needs to think about now is a dad who was whacked out on drugs.

Marina yelps. "What?"

Mary Alice smiles sadly. "Don't worry about it, Rina. I don't have any illusions about the sixties. Or my father."

chapter NINE

HIPPIE CHAI

2 quarts milk (goat or soy milk is best—but cow's milk will
   work for those who are still entrenched in "Babylon")

4-inch piece fresh ginger root, peeled and crushed

1 1/2 tablespoons coarsely crushed whole cardamom pods

1 tablespoon coarsely crushed whole cloves

1 cinnamon stick

2 tablespoons honey or brown sugar

Instructions:

1. Bring milk to a boil over high heat. Then reduce to a
   medium simmer.

2. Add ginger, cardamom, cloves, and cinnamon. Simmer
   10–15 minutes. Be sure to stir every so often.

3. Add honey or brown sugar to taste.

4. Strain and serve hot from a teapot.

Makes 8 cups or 6 (12 ounce) servings.

HOMEMADE YOGURT

1/2 teaspoon unflavored gelatin

Water (as instructed below)

1 tablespoon sugar

3 cups powdered milk

1 (12 ounce) can evaporated milk

2 tablespoons plain yogurt (with live cultures)

Instructions

1. Preheat oven to 275 degrees.
2. Dissolve gelatin in 1 cup boiling water. Add sugar and stir until mixture is dissolved. Cool.
3. Mix powdered milk into 3 cups water.
4. In a large glass ovenproof bowl, stir together evaporated milk and 2 cups lukewarm water. Add powered milk mixture and gelatin mixture. Then add yogurt. Stir together well. Cover.
5. Put covered bowl in oven and turn off heat. Let it remain in oven 10 hours—or overnight.
6. Flavor with fruit or vanilla, if desired.

Makes 2 quarts.

May 20, 1967

NEW YORK—Tensions were high earlier today as a group of antiwar protesters infiltrated a march organized by veterans to show support for troops serving in Vietnam. The group of infiltrators, led by activist Abbie Hoffman, displayed flowers as a symbol of what they are calling "Flower Power."

●

"By walking softly upon the Earth, we show our respect for all life," explained the barefoot young woman who had introduced herself as Willow. Draped in a long dress of white muslin, she led Ali and Denny through the back door of the old farmhouse as they continued their tour of Avalon—an "intentional community" in the Missouri Ozarks.

While the trio picked their way along a dusty path, Willow expounded on the philosophy of the commune. "Here at Avalon we believe it is obscene to disturb even the smallest created thing. For grains of sand make mountains, and atoms, infinity. By living in balance and freedom, we satisfy the true longing of our souls."

The girl turned away in a cloud of billowy fabric. Ali wrinkled her brow and silently mouthed to Denny, "What?"

Denny winked in response and put a finger to his lips. A new way of thinking was just one of the things he and Ali would have to get used to at Avalon. The primitive facilities were another.

They has just finished their orientation to the commune in what was referred to as the Rec Room—an old school bus with the bench seats replaced by floor pillows and grubby sleeping bags. The leader of the community, a small man with dark, piercing eyes whom residents called Levi, explained that the ramshackle farmhouse was only to be used for sleeping and cooking. Meals for the ten residents were served in a converted tool shed called the Dining

Hall. When Ali, now six months pregnant, asked for directions to the bathroom, Levi's response seemed to shock even Denny's nature-loving wife.

"We believe that indoor plumbing keeps the environment captive to a corrupt system," Levi explained, taking a sip of the spicy Chai one of the women had served along with a dish of Homemade Yogurt sweetened with strawberries. "We free ourselves from the constraints of a bourgeois society by living in harmony with nature."

Ali's jaw dropped. "So there's no running water out here? Not even for cooking? Or laundry?"

"We have a well. And a hand pump." With a tranquil smile, Levi suggested Willow begin the couple's tour of the compound at the Waste Renewal Center. In other words, the outhouse.

This new life would definitely take some getting used to, Denny thought as they continued their tour of the property. But isn't that what they wanted? To get back to the land and raise their child in harmony with nature?

"So when is your baby due?" asked Willow, looking over her shoulder at Ali, who was wearing a smocked maternity top.

"At the end of August," answered Denny proudly.

Ali smiled. "You'd think he was the one giving birth."

"I'll be right there with you, babe." Denny placed his hand on Ali's swollen abdomen.

"We'll have to see what the doctor says about that." She laughed.

Willow stopped short on the path and turned around. "Don't worry about a doctor. We have a midwife here at Avalon who can deliver your baby."

Ali bit her lip. "Right here? Not at a hospital?"

"There's no need. Natalie has great hands. She'll catch your little one." Willow continued along the path.

Ali caught Denny's eye. He shrugged and motioned her to follow Willow. There was plenty of time to think about who would deliver their baby. Right now they needed to find their place at Avalon.

June 18, 1967

MONTEREY, CALIF.—Today marks the end of the three-day pop festival at the Monterey Fairgrounds in Northern California. Thirty-one bands performed for a crowd of mostly young people that swelled to 200,000. Performers included Janis Joplin, The Byrds, Country Joe and the Fish, The Grateful Dead, The Jimi Hendrix Experience, Jefferson Airplane, The Mamas and The Papas, The Steve Miller Band, Ravi Shakar, Simon and Garfunkel, The Who . . .

"Come on, baby," Denny slurred. "It's like the Beatles say. 'All you need is love.'"

With no set schedule for the men and an abundance of recreational chemicals, Denny now rarely got up before noon. He had awakened earlier and looked out the window to see Ali hunched over, weeding the massive organic garden she had put in shortly after they arrived at Avalon. But the pang of guilt he felt about not helping her was overshadowed by his throbbing head.

Gotta get to bed earlier.

Denny had helped dig up the unyielding clay soil, but after seeing how little the other men contributed to the functioning of Avalon, he quickly lost interest in the project. Obviously, chicks had different roles at the commune. It wouldn't be right to upset the order.

"Come on, Den, my back is killing me." Ali stretched and rubbed the small of her back, straining the T-shirt covering her swollen belly. "I need you to go into town for groceries."

"Anything for you, babe." Denny leered. "But first . . ." He grabbed her wrist and drew her toward him.

Ali twisted away from his grasp. "Not now. If you don't go get the groceries, I won't have time to make dinner this afternoon."

Denny scowled and pulled an old T-shirt over his head. "Your loss, babe. Give me some bread for the store."

"I don't have any money."

"Then how do you expect me to buy groceries? The guy at the A&P isn't likely to give credit to a longhair, is he?"

"What about the check your sister sent us last week?"

Denny fastened the waist of his worn Levi's. "I lent it to Joe."

"Joe? What for? To replenish his stash?"

"It's none of your business. The whole point of Avalon is to share what we have and live off the land."

Ali shook her head. "Feeding Joe's drug habit is not my idea of living off the land."

Denny sat on the edge of the bed to tie his desert boots. "You know, Ali, you're getting to be a drag."

"Denny! Look at me!" A tear slipped down her cheek. "I'm going to have our child in two months. I've worked my fingers to the bone trying to keep things together, and all you do is lie around with Levi and the rest of the burnouts here."

"Ali, come on. You know that's not—"

"Yes, it is. And the only medical care I've gotten is from Natalie. It's like you don't care about me or the baby." Splotches from her tears peppered the front of her T-shirt.

Denny drew his sobbing wife into his arms. "Come on, babe. You know I love you. And I can't wait to meet our little tadpole." He pulled back and used his thumb to wipe away Ali's tears. "I'm sorry. Give me another chance?"

●

August 30, 1967

SAN FRANCISCO—It's not over yet, but many are already calling 1967 the "Summer of Love." Thousands of young people have flocked to the Haight-Ashbury district of the city for what they consider a personal pilgrimage. They are buoyed by the fervency of their cause, their great numbers, and the call of musician John Phillips and others proclaiming, "If you come to San Francisco, be sure to wear some flowers in your hair."

●

"Denny, I think my water broke. We need to go to the hospital."

Ali had shaken Denny awake from a sound sleep. He pushed up on one elbow in the double bed he had built in Camille so he and Ali could have some privacy. As more people joined the commune, it was no use trying to get any sleep in the farmhouse.

Denny also didn't want to make a big deal about his and Ali's decision to have the baby at the hospital instead of letting Natalie do the delivery. Ali overheard one of the women whispering that a teenage girl and her baby had died last year during a breach birth. Levi's response to their concerns was a bleary, "Don't let your reality get in the way of your perception."

Levi was so stoned these days, Denny wondered if he would even notice Ali had given birth. "Yeah, Levi, don't let your reality get in the way of your perceptions."

"What did you say, Den?" Ali's voice from outside the van made Denny realize he had spoken his thoughts aloud.

Denny climbed out of the van and took his wife's elbow. "Nothing, babe. Let me help you into the front seat."

●

$\mathcal{M}$ary Alice, is this you?" Jess picks up a faded Polaroid from the box of memorabilia of a bearded young man in a hospital gown holding an infant. He is smiling broadly at the baby while a young woman with long blond hair looks up from a hospital bed.

Mary Alice takes the photo from Jess. "That's my mom, so I assume it's me."

We're still sitting at the table in the van. It's actually quite nice. Especially with mellow tunes from *The Best of Bread* playing in the background. When Marina discovered a black vinyl case filled with old eight-track tapes, she had insisted on hooking the van's battery up to the one in her car so she could try out the tape player. None of us argued, knowing it would be pointless. When Marina has her mind set, it's set in stone.

Now, sitting at the table listening to the music, I have to admit Marina was right. The nostalgic tunes lighten the mood, and everyone seems more relaxed.

Except for me, that is. I was obsessed with thoughts of cannoli.

After we'd finished lunch, Marina had asked if anyone was up for dessert. I was almost beside myself when everyone else begged off, saying they were stuffed.

"But Marina made cannoli," I'd said. "She went to a lot of trouble and—"

"Don't worry, Liz." Marina gave me what I will go to my grave insisting was an evil eye. "I can always take them home."

The rest of the group acquiesced to this plan while I returned Marina's malevolent gaze. She knew I'd be too embarrassed to admit I was the only one who wanted dessert. That I'd suffer in silence rather than admit I'd been thinking about that cannoli all morning.

Marina has made it her personal project this year to "toughen me up" and teach me to stand up for myself. I am, by nature, a peacemaker. I don't like to make waves. But Marina insists there's a rebellious streak in me, and she takes every opportunity to fan the flame.

This must be why she's so adept at getting criminals to confess.

So here I am, sitting in a 1963 Volkswagen minibus with faded orange shag carpeting on the walls and an eight-track player under the dash. And all I can think about are the twelve cannolis sitting in a cooler in Marina's convertible. I am going to get her for this.

"It don't matter to me, if you really feel that . . ." Marina and Jess close their eyes and sing along with lyrics to the song that saturated the airwaves in the late sixties.

Did she pick this song on purpose?

"M.A., this isn't you." Kelly interrupts my pastry dreams by holding up the Polaroid. "It says on the back *Denny, Maya, and me.* Who's Maya?"

The expression on Mary Alice's face makes me forget all about the cannolis.

chAPTER TEN

AVALON RICE AND LENTIL STEW

1 cup (1/2 pound) dried brown lentils, picked over and rinsed

1 1/2 pounds Swiss chard, trimmed and chopped

1 large potato, peeled and cut into medium-sized chunks

1 large turnip, peeled and cut into medium-sized chunks

2 cups hot water

Salt and pepper to taste

1 red bell pepper, chopped

1 large onion, chopped

1 teaspoon chopped garlic

1/2 cup olive oil

1 (16 ounce) can diced tomatoes or 2 large tomatoes, peeled and chopped

1 cup medium-grain rice

Instructions

1. In a Dutch oven, cover lentils, Swiss chard, potato, and turnip with 2 cups hot water. Add salt and pepper.

2. Bring to a boil, reduce heat, and simmer 20 minutes.

3. Meanwhile, sauté red pepper, onion, and garlic in olive oil until soft. Add tomato and cook 5 minutes more before adding to Dutch oven.

4. Simmer stew 40 minutes over low heat.

5. Add rice and cook until rice has absorbed the liquid—about 20 minutes.

Serves 6–8.

VEGGIE FRIED RICE

Olive or vegetable oil

Garlic, chopped

Onions, chopped

Pot of cooked white rice

Bowl of about equal size (as rice pot) of fresh vegetables,
cut up (whatever kinds of vegetables you like: asparagus,
mushrooms, broccoli, red, yellow, and green peppers,
cauliflower, green onions, green and yellow zucchini squash,
thinly sliced carrots, peas, hot peppers, etc.)

Soy sauce

Instructions

1. Coat a large frying pan with olive or vegetable oil. Add garlic
   and onion. Cook 2 minutes.
2. Add vegetables and sauté until tender.
3. Add cooked rice and soy sauce to taste. Mix thoroughly and
   sauté until it looks done—about 5 minutes.

APPLE COMPOTE

2 tart apples (such as Granny Smith)

3 tablespoons butter

4–5 tablespoons brown sugar

1/2 cup sherry

1/2 cup raisins

Instructions

1. Peel and core apples. Cut into thick slices.
2. Melt butter in a heavy pan. Add apples and cook just until fork tender (not mushy).
3. Mix in brown sugar until it dissolves, creating a smooth caramel sauce.
4. Add sherry and raisins.
5. Cook until hot and bubbly. Mixture will thicken as it stands.
6. Keep warm until serving time. Serve alone or over rice for dessert.

October 20, 1967

OAKLAND, CALIF.—The biggest demonstration yet against U.S. involvement in the Vietnam War was held here today. An estimated 4,000 people poured onto the streets to demonstrate in a fifth day of massive protests as part of what is being called "Stop the Draft Week"—a nationwide initiative which has seen peace marches in cities across the United States. The city was brought to a standstill as protesters built barricades across roads to prevent buses carrying recruits to the Army's induction center. Police reinforcements came in from San Francisco as the protests turned violent. Demonstrators, many wearing helmets and holding plywood shields, overturned cars and threw bottles, tin cans, and rocks at the police. Protests are expected to move to Washington, D.C., tomorrow.

●

"Hey there, Baby Maya!" Willow picked up the sleeping child from a thick quilt on the floor and began to twirl around the long pine table in Avalon's make-shift Dining Hall. Jarred from her afternoon nap, the little girl began to howl. "What's the hassle, kitty cat? You sound just like your mama now."

Denny lifted his head from the sagging couch across the room where he was lounging with several of the other men while they listened to Mick Jagger belt out "Dandelion" on the radio. "What's the matter with you, Willow? Why'd you have to go and wake her up?"

"I thought the kid needed a little fun, Denny. Your old lady is always so uptight. Maya needs some good karma."

Ali pushed open the door to the Dining Hall with her hip, burdened by a large pot of Avalon Rice and Lentil Stew. Her eyes shot immediately to the screaming baby in Willow's arms. "Denny, what happened? You said you would watch Maya while I was in the kitchen."

"It's cool, babe. She just woke up."

Ali rushed to the long pine table and set down the heavy pot. She took the hysterical baby from Willow, who was holding her with outstretched arms— like a smelly rag.

"It's all right, sweetness. Mama's here." The baby's frantic cries soon softened to a whimper.

Denny got up from the sofa and ambled across the room to peer into his daughter's face. "See?" He rubbed the baby's tender cheek with a calloused finger. "She just missed her mom. Didn't you, pretty girl?"

Ali sighed. "Denny, you're going to have to carry the rest of the food over from the kitchen for me. There's still a bowl of Veggie Fried Rice and some Apple Compote. I'll stay here with Maya."

"Don't forget your apron, Den!" said Joe, lifting up the battered straw hat that had been covering his eyes as he reclined on a pile of multicolored floor pillows.

Levi laughed from his perch in a large rattan chair suspended from the rafters by a heavy chain. "Yeah, we all know that a chick's work is never done."

Willow giggled.

Denny clenched his hands into fists at his sides. "Lay off, man."

Ali, ears burning red, gave Willow a sharp look and whirled to face her husband's tormentors. "I am so sick of your hypocrisy! You preach peace, love, and equality. But when it comes time to do any work, you're too lazy or too wasted to do your share. It's *pathetic*." Ali turned back to Denny. "I'm splitting. Maya needs a nap—and so do I."

"Come on, wait a minute, Al." Denny moved toward the retreating form of his wife and daughter.

Willow took a step sideways and blocked his path with her ballerina-like body. "Don't worry, baby. I'll take over in the kitchen for your old lady." In a husky tone, she whispered in his ear, "I appreciate a good man."

Denny stood in stunned silence as he watched Willow leave the Dining Hall. *What just happened?*

He heard the scrape of a chair as Levi took his place at the head of the table.

"Some bad vibes coming from your old lady, man."

"Yeah, a real bummer." Joe drew out the rough pine bench at Levi's end of the table and sat down.

Denny perched on the outside of the bench with his back to the two men. He stared out the grimy window into the deepening twilight.

What did Ali want from him? She was the one who wanted to raise their baby in the country. Who wanted to live off the land. Well, here they were, and she still wasn't happy.

Denny knew it was harder now that Maya was part of the picture. Ali didn't sleep well in such close quarters—squeezed in the back of Camille with the baby between them. But he didn't get much sleep either. Did she think he couldn't hear the kid screaming right next to his ear?

And he was tired of hearing his wife complain he wasn't doing his share to take care of Maya. Ali was nursing, so he couldn't feed her. When Maya cried, she always wanted Ali to soothe her. And there were some things you couldn't expect a guy to do—like rinsing out dirty diapers in the creek.

"Man!" Denny swiveled and hit the table, shaking the mismatched crockery laid out for dinner. "What does that chick want from me?"

Levi leaned forward, elbows on the table. "You know, Den, maybe Ali isn't down with the Dream. All that we're trying to do here at Avalon to make a better society. Some chicks are too tied to Babylon to break free."

"No, Ali's down with the Dream, man. I know that. It's just with Maya—"

Levi put his hand up to stop Denny's words. "I dig what you're trying to say, bro. But it's like Ken Kesey says, 'You're either on the bus—or you're off the bus.'"

Denny rubbed his face with his hands. Maybe Levi had a point.

"The other chicks seem to dig the whole Earth Mother thing." Joe lowered his voice as the door to the Dining Hall opened. "Take Willow. That girl's got karma . . ."

Denny grinned as Willow walked through the door in her thin muslin dress carrying a bowl of fried rice and vegetables. "Karma, huh?"

Joe leered at the young woman moving around the table, arranging bowls and serving utensils. "I don't care what you call it, but she's got it. And I'm digging it."

"I'm down with that," Denny said in a hoarse voice as he caught Willow's sideways glance on her way out the door.

●

October 21, 1967
WASHINGTON, D.C.—A crowd that some estimate at 70,000 antiwar protestors stormed the Pentagon today in demonstrations that resulted in 647 arrests. Large numbers of young men burned their draft cards, which is an illegal act under a law passed by Congress two years ago. Recent polls suggest that American support for the war in Vietnam is declining steadily as well as support for the administration of President Lyndon B. Johnson.

●

Denny leaned over and punched the off button on Camille's radio. "I should have been there!" He slammed the van's door just as Joe came down the path.

"Hey man, what's the hassle? Your old lady still not cuttin' you any slack?"

"Yeah . . . that." Denny raked his fingers through his shoulder-length hair. Things between him and Ali had been strained since the incident in the Dining Hall the previous night. In fact, Ali had never even showed up for dinner. When he came back to Camille later that night, she and Maya were already asleep. Or at least Ali pretended to be sleeping.

This morning, Ali had gotten up early, fed Maya, and fastened the baby snugly into the little front carrier she had made. Denny's attempts to make conversation were met with one-word answers.

"Yeah."

"Hmmm."

"Uh-huh."

This wasn't at all like his wife. But Denny was at a loss about how to deal with her. Willow advised giving her some "space."

Chicks! Why do things have to be so complicated?

Denny looked at Joe. "Ali just needs some space, and things will be cool."

"I feel for ya, man. She's been a real drag lately."

Denny chose to ignore the comment. "We shoulda gone to D.C. I just heard on the radio that seventy thousand marched on the Pentagon. I feel like I'm missing the Revolution down here in the sticks."

"I know what you mean. Levi told me Abbie Hoffman tried to exorcise the Pentagon."

"You're kidding! What'd he do?"

"He lined up a bunch of hippies and got 'em sitting lotus-style so they surrounded the building. They were supposed to sing and chant until the building levitated and turned orange. You know, to drive out the evil spirits and end the war in Vietnam."

"Far-out. What happened?"

"Nothing. But it was a cool idea."

Denny heard a twig snap.

Willow walked out of the woods into the clearing. How long had she been there? he wondered.

The tall young woman stared at Denny with her huge gray eyes. Denny couldn't take his eyes off her as she walked slowly toward him.

Joe grinned. "Hey man, like Abbie says, 'The first duty of a revolutionary is to get away with it.'"

*D*o you think a mood ring really works?" I slip the silver ring with the dark glass stone on my right index finger. "Whenever I put one on, the stone is always black."

I had found the ring in a rusted Maxwell House coffee can I dug out of one of the cabinets in the van while Jess, Kelly, and Mary Alice drove to the office to use the restroom. The can contained a treasure trove of memorabilia, including a medallion fashioned from a wooden peace symbol strung on a piece of rawhide, a keychain with the mathematical symbol for infinity, and a variety of political buttons.

Marina looks up from the stack of eight-track tapes she is sorting on the floor of the storage unit. "Black means you're anxious about something, Lizzie. A mood ring always turns deep blue on me. The sign of passion."

"Of course it would," I mumble.

Lucy is sifting through a pile of photos that were stored in a red and black Dingo boot box under the driver's seat. "All a mood ring tells you is if your hands are warm or cold. Black means you have cold hands."

Marina pushes herself up from the concrete floor. "My point exactly. Warm hands—warm heart."

"Actually, the saying is, 'Cold hands—warm heart.' So I guess I'm the passionate one." I hold my hand with the mood ring up to prove my point.

Marina folds her arms across her chest. "Oh really? Then how come the cannolis are still sitting in my cooler?"

I narrow my eyes at Marina. "Why would I want a cannoli when I'm *not hungry?*"

Marina holds my stare. "You tell me."

In my head, I know Marina thinks she is doing me a favor by goading me. It's all part of her "teach Liz to stand up for herself" program. But inside, I'm fuming. I will not let her bully me—even if she thinks it's for my own good.

Apparently sensing a face-off, Lucy changes the subject. "I need your opinion, ladies."

I don't want to be the first one to look away. "What is it, Lucy?" I ask, keeping my eyes locked on Marina's.

Marina is silent. As if daring me to break eye contact. A smile plays at the corner of her mouth.

I see Lucy in my peripheral vision, furrows creasing her normally smooth brow. "Most of these photos have Maya written on the back of them. *Maya—six months. Maya at the creek—nine months.* Doesn't it seem a little strange that Mary Alice's dad had all of these pictures of this Maya—and we haven't found a single photo of Mary Alice?"

"You're thinking M.A.'s dad has another family stashed somewhere," says Marina without blinking an eye.

How does she do it? My eyes are already getting tired—and I'm blinking. Frequently. But I am determined not to let her win. Blink or no blink.

"As far as I know, my dad may very well have another family 'stashed' somewhere, as you so colorfully put it, Marina."

Marina and I both jump at Mary Alice's voice. She is standing with Jess and Kelly in the entrance to the storage unit. Their frames are backlit by the afternoon sun.

How long have they been there? Could they tell Marina and I were having a staring contest—straight out of junior high? If so, Kelly will never let me hear the end of it. She still teases me about being the only woman in the school's history to be fired as Cookie Mom.

And if my kids ever get wind of this . . .

Marina's voice pulls me back from the abyss of paranoia to reality. "M.A., I didn't mean—"

"Don't feel bad, Marina. I'm the one who should apologize for keeping so many secrets. It's all going to come out eventually."

I take a step toward Mary Alice. "What's going to come out?"

Again all thoughts of cannolis or staring contests are whisked away by the mystery unfolding before me. A mystery surrounding a woman I would have picked as the least mysterious person I know. And the pool of mysterious people in my circle is pretty shallow anyway.

Mary Alice takes a deep breath. "First of all, Mary Alice is not my real name."

chAPTER
ELEVEN

MILLET CASSEROLE

2 cups cooked millet*

6 green onions, sliced

1 large carrot, grated

8 ounces mushrooms, sliced

1 small green pepper, diced

2 medium tomatoes, diced

1 cup chopped broccoli

Basil, oregano, thyme to taste

1 cup grated cheese

Instructions

1. Combine all ingredients except for cheese.

2. Put in a well-greased 9x13-inch baking dish. Sprinkle cheese on top.

3. Bake at 350 degrees until hot—approximately 30 minutes.

* Millet can be found in most health-food stores. Cooking millet is similar to cooking rice. Use one part millet to two parts water. (Add less water if you prefer a lighter, fluffier texture.) Add salt if desired. Cover and simmer over low heat until liquid is absorbed—usually about 30 minutes. Millet can easily be substituted for rice in other recipes.

HOMEMADE PEANUT BUTTER

1 cup shelled roasted peanuts

2–3 tablespoons peanut or safflower oil

Instructions

1. Put peanuts in bowl of food processor and process on high. Add just enough oil during processing to get a smooth consistency. (This can also be done using a mortar and pestle combined with a lot of elbow grease.)
2. Store in refrigerator in an airtight container. Use within a couple of weeks.

Makes 1 1/4 cups.

January 31, 1968

SAIGON—In a show of military might, North Vietnamese and Vietcong forces swept down upon several key cities and provinces in South Vietnam, including the capital, Saigon. Many in Washington are questioning the U.S. Defense Department's assessment of the war and have stated publicly that the "light at the end of the tunnel" appears nowhere in sight.

●

Ali and Denny huddled against a building across from the busy Missouri State Capitol in Jefferson City. Ali had wrapped Maya in three blankets in an effort to shield her from the winter wind. They had been working the corner for more than an hour with little to show for their efforts.

A stab of guilt cut through Denny as he looked at his wife's wind-burned cheeks. "How much do we have so far?"

"Just three dollars and some change." Ali folded back a corner of the tattered blanket and peeked at the sleeping baby. "Denny, we can't keep Maya out here much longer. I'm afraid she's going to get a cold."

"We can't quit with just three bucks." Denny blew into his ungloved hands and rubbed them together. "Here comes someone now."

Denny pasted a smile on his face and stepped away from the wall to the middle of the sidewalk. A middle-aged man carrying a briefcase strode toward him.

"Hey man, can you spare some change?"

The man glared at Denny, making him aware of his long hair and unkempt beard, then strode by without saying a word.

"Hey man, what's your problem?" Denny shouted after the man. Less than a minute ago, he'd been hoping for a handout. Now his hands were balled into tight fists.

The businessman stopped on the sidewalk, pausing briefly before he turned to face Denny. "Listen closely, *man*. From what I can see, I'm not the one who has the problem. Am I?"

As the businessman turned away again, Denny yelled, "Well, at least I haven't sold out to The System. Go on back to Babylon!" He shoved his hands into the front pockets of his patched Levi's and leaned up against the wall next to Ali.

Denny hated panhandling, and he hated asking Ali to come with him. He could just imagine what Ali's dad—or his own hardworking father—would think if they knew how he, Ali, and the baby were really living. But what choice did he have? Now that tourist season was over in the Ozarks, there wasn't a market for his woodworking. And the locals had no use for the longhairs who lived at Avalon, and they weren't about to buy any of his things. At least once a month he and Ali would wake up to the racket of a bunch of rednecks throwing bottles out their pickups and shouting, "Hippies, go home!"

"Denny, let's go. We're not getting anywhere here."

Denny gritted his teeth. "We would be doing better if you weren't so uptight."

"What's that supposed to mean?"

"I told you it's important to make eye contact. Oil the Machine. You didn't even look at that guy."

Ali clenched her jaw and snuggled the baby closer. "This is so humiliating."

Ignoring his wife's comment, Denny stepped away from the wall. "Here comes another one."

A worried-looking mother, clutching the hand of a preschooler, edged as far as she could on the sidewalk without stepping into the street in an apparent effort to avoid Denny.

Denny smiled. "Ma'am, could you spare some change?"

The woman stopped and looked nervously around. "I don't know. My husband says—"

"It's just that, you see, my wife and little girl here"—Denny looked back at Ali and Maya—"we need to buy some baby food and stuff."

The two mothers' eyes met in silent understanding. "I guess I can help out a little." The woman opened her pocketbook.

Ali averted her eyes, but not before Denny saw her wipe away a tear.

"Thank you, ma'am." He took the two bills and shoved them in the front pocket of his jeans. "Let's split," he told Ali.

Ali and Denny walked the two short blocks to where they had parked Camille. After buying some gas and a sack of millet from the Whole Foods store, Denny turned left on the road that would lead them back to Avalon.

"I was thinking . . . how about I write a cookbook?" Ali handed Denny one of the Homemade Peanut Butter and honey sandwiches she had packed for lunch. "I could call it *50 Ways to Serve Millet—and Live to Tell about It.*"

"Why do you always have to be such a bummer?"

"*I'm* a bummer?" A familiar red began to color Ali's ears. "I'm a bummer because I don't like begging on street corners for food? I'm a bummer because I want Maya to see a doctor when she's sick instead of a so-called midwife who is wasted half the time? I'm a bummer because I'm tired of eating Millet Casserole?"

Maya began to whimper. Ali made soothing sounds as she adjusted her clothing to nurse the baby.

After a few minutes, Denny broke the strained silence. "So you want to sell out? Go back to Rock Port? Want me to get a job with my old man selling insurance?"

"Come on, Denny, you know I love you. But I'm sick of the way we're living. All of it. The dirt. The cold. The panhandling. Even the people."

"I thought you were getting along better with the women."

Ali glared at Denny before shifting her gaze out the window. "It's not just the women any more. You never know what drugged-out lunatics Levi is going to bring back from one of his 'voyages' these days."

Denny continued driving in silence.

"I'm sorry, Den, but you promised me Eden. This is Hell."

●

April 5, 1968

MEMPHIS—The Rev. Dr. Martin Luther King Jr., who preached nonviolence and racial brotherhood, was fatally shot today as he stood on his hotel balcony by a distant gunman who raced away and escaped. King was in Memphis to lead a march of sanitation workers protesting low wages and poor working conditions. Four thousand National Guard troops were ordered into Memphis by Gov. Buford Ellington after the 39-year-old Nobel Prize-winning civil rights leader died. A curfew was imposed on the shocked city of 550,000 inhabitants, 40 percent of whom are Negro.

●

"Hey man, Bruno's takin' the boys to Memphis," Joe announced, referring to the leader of a group of Hells Angels that had been camping at Avalon for the last week. "I'm goin' along. You in?"

Denny dropped the copy of the *I-Ching* he had been reading and jumped up from the old flowered sofa he and Joe had found dumpster-diving. "When are you leaving?"

"Now. Camille could use a little road trip, couldn't she?"

"Sorry, bro, Camille's outta gas."

"No problem, I've got enough bread to get us there. We can worry about gettin' back later."

Denny shook his head. "I don't know, man. Ali's in town with Natalie, I can't leave without—"

"Leave her a note. The Movement's callin', man. You gonna sit out forever?"

●

April 6, 1968

MEMPHIS—Several thousand members of the Tennessee National Guard are patrolling the city in an effort to ward off violence following the death of Dr. Martin Luther King Jr. President Lyndon Johnson said he was "shocked and saddened" by the civil rights leader's death. "I ask every citizen to reject the blind violence that has taken Dr. King, who lived by nonviolence." A dusk-to-dawn curfew has been ordered throughout the city to ward off disturbances.

●

Denny and Joe didn't reach the outskirts of Memphis until about nine o'clock Saturday night—two days after Dr. King was shot. Although the city was only a six-hour drive from Avalon, Bruno had led the caravan on a detour to see some longhairs he knew near Cape Girardeau, Missouri. What was supposed to be a quick stop turned into an all-night party in an A-frame on the outskirts of the Southeast Missouri State campus.

Bruno and the rest of the Hells Angels didn't come down from the night of revelry until late the next day. By then they had all but forgotten the reason for the trip and decided to continue the party through the weekend. Their hosts weren't about to object.

"Come on, boys," Bruno had drawled in his North Carolina accent earlier that afternoon. "Just bag the scene in Memphis. There's plenty to keep y'all busy here."

The rusty-bearded outlaw grabbed the wrist of a bleary-eyed girl walking across the room and pulled her down in his lap. "What's your name, girl? Starshine or Rainbow?"

Joe laughed and plopped down in a lime green beanbag chair. "I'm down with hangin' out here, man. I say go with the flow."

Denny couldn't believe what he was hearing. He hadn't wanted to stop last night, but Joe convinced him it wasn't a good idea to hassle with Bruno. Now Joe wanted to bag the whole reason for the road trip to hang out with this bunch of burnouts.

"What about the Movement, bro?" Denny's frustration and anger grew.

"That's the whole idea, boy." Bruno blew a ring of smoke in the girl's face. "We're not gonna move. We're gonna groove."

The young woman giggled.

●

After much discussion, Joe reluctantly agreed to continue on to Memphis on one condition—Denny would do the driving. Joe wanted to sleep in the back of Camille.

After all the activity of the night before, Denny was enjoying the solitude of the drive. As he was mellowing out to "Scarborough Fair"—Simon and Garfunkel's latest release on the radio—his headlights illuminated a series of barricades on the road ahead.

"Bro! Wake up! I think it's the fuzz!" Denny rapped on the wooden sheet he'd built to divide the front cab from the back of Camille.

The little panel slid open, and Joe's face appeared. "What's goin' down, man?"

"I don't know yet. You holding?"

"No man, I'm clean."

Denny breathed a sigh of relief at his friend's answer as a burly Marine, dressed in fatigues and carrying an M-16, motioned for him to pull Camille to the side of the road.

A military transport truck was parked across the two-lane highway blocking both lanes of southbound traffic. A group of guardsmen milled around nearby.

Denny rolled down his window. "What's the problem, man?"

"The city is under a curfew," said the officer. "No vehicles are allowed in after dark."

"That's bogus, man! You can't stop me from driving on a state highway." Denny had come too far to let some fascist-playing GI Joe stand in his way.

"Sir, I am under orders by the governor of the State of Tennessee to secure this road. You will have to turn around."

"Don't give me any of that military propaganda. This is a free country, man. You can't keep us out."

The soldier took a deep breath and moved closer to the window. "Just watch me. *Man.* By the way, I don't see you putting your rear on the line for any of those freedoms you keep talking about. So listen very carefully." The guardsman took a step back—his automatic weapon in the ready position. "Turn around that bucket of bolts you're driving and head back to the freak show you came from. *Dig?*"

●

*Y*ou could have knocked me over with a feather.

This old cliché was never truer as I stand open-mouthed while my friends pepper Mary Alice with questions so quickly that I can hardly keep up.

Kelly: "What do you mean Mary Alice isn't your name?"

Marina: "Are you part of the witness protection program?"

Jess: "What about Craig? Your kids? Are they part of this too?"

Lucy: "Maybe she's not supposed to talk about it. Are you?"

Back to Marina: "Yeah, so now you have to kill us, right?"

My friends' jaws drop along with my own as all eyes turn to Marina, then back to Mary Alice. Or whatever her name is. I fight simultaneous urges to pull out my reporter's notebook—or run for my life.

Mary Alice laughs, breaking the tension. "I'm sorry, but the thought of me as some mob informant is hysterical. The truth is far less exciting."

I let out the breath I hadn't realized I was holding. Unconsciously waiting for "an offer I couldn't refuse," I guess.

Now my curiosity is at full volume. "So if Mary Alice isn't your real name, then what—"

Mary Alice interrupts me. "It's not that big of a deal. My parents named me Maya Alice. Alice after my mom—and Maya probably because it sounded exotic."

Jess gives Mary Alice's shoulder a squeeze. "I think it's beautiful. What does it mean?"

"I have no idea. And I never cared to find out. I hated the name Maya. The kids at school used to call me the 'hippie chick.'"

Lucy shakes her head slowly from her perch on the running board of the van. "Kids can be so cruel."

Mary Alice straightens her shoulders. "So when I went away to college, I had my first name changed to Mary. My mother's never gotten over it."

"Does she still call you Maya?" I ask.

Mary Alice chuckles softly. "Of course."

Kelly folds her arms across her chest. "So that's it? You just didn't like your name so you changed it?"

"That's it. It was my first real act of rebellion."

"Well, your revolutionary days are over." Marina passes out plastic trash bags from a big roll. "Help us go through this stuff. I've got plans tonight."

●

*M*y kids better not try and change their names," I grouse. "Being able to pick your child's name is one of the spoils of motherhood."

Lucy grins and takes the box of magazines I'm holding out to her.

With Kelly as the foreman, the six of us have formed a makeshift assembly line to clear out the van. Marina, the most agile of our group, is crouched on the floor of the van, dragging stuff out of the built-in cabinets and cubbies. I hand what she ferrets out to Lucy, who is standing by a big trash can lined with a heavy duty plastic bag. Her job is to decide whether to immediately dump the contents in the trash or pass it to Jess and M.A. to sort further.

Kelly has set up three piles to make sorting as simple as possible.

Save.

Sell.

Scrapbook.

When I questioned her about the wisdom of the *Scrapbook* pile, she gave me one of those *you wouldn't understand* looks I recognize from my children. I've become somewhat of an expert of interpreting these facial expressions perfected by my kids. I can identify the *what were you thinking?* look and the eye-rolling *whatever* without hesitation. But after today, I'm beginning to wonder if Kelly taught my kids their repertoire of surly nonverbal communication. After all, we were in a babysitting co-op together.

Before my suspicions can fully root, Lucy interrupts my thoughts. "I always wanted to change my name when I was growing up. I got so sick of kids asking, 'Hey Lucy, where's Charlie Brown?'"

"So, is the doctor in?" I quip. "I've got my nickel."

"Very funny," says Lucy as she tosses a cigar box full of candle stubs in the trash can.

"Sorry, I couldn't help myself." I smile and hand her another box. "I never really liked my name either. I remember thinking Elizabeth was so boring. Why couldn't my parents have named me something cool?"

"Like what?" asks Marina, reaching up to pull a plastic container from an upper cabinet.

"For a long time, I wanted to be named CeCe—after this character in a serial that used to run in *Tiger Beat* magazine. I loved that name."

Marina laughs. "CeCe? Now I've heard everything."

Kelly's face appears in the opening between the front seat and the rear compartment. "There were two kids named Kelly in my class all through elementary school. And one was a boy. The happiest day of my life was when I found out that kid was moving to Minnesota."

Marina stretches her right arm across her chest. "Some dweeb in fifth grade came up to me in the lunch line and asked, 'Hey Marina, where should I park my boat?'"

Fool, I thought. *That kid probably had no idea of the chutzpah hiding behind those long, black eyelashes.*

Lucy looks up from the plastic tub of old candles she has just dumped in the trash. "Did you let him get away with it?"

Marina snorts. "Yeah, right. I pointed over his shoulder and asked, 'Is that a good spot?' When he looked away, I kicked him in the shin with my new Famolare platforms. Never had any more problems."

I can't help but laugh. "Marina, you may drive me crazy—but you're still my hero."

"Duh." Marina turns away, her long black ponytail bobbing.

"Anyone ever hear of *The Realist*?" Jess holds up a yellowed magazine from the box she and Mary Alice are sorting through. "I'm thinking they might be worth something on eBay."

I hop out of the van and cross to where Jess and Mary Alice are sitting cross-legged on the floor. "I know that magazine. The guy who used to put it out spoke to our class in journalism school. Paul Krassner."

"He's listed as publisher." Jess points to a name on the inside cover. "I'm impressed, Lizzie."

I take the magazine from Jess. "I remember because I saw him on Conan O'Brien a couple of years ago. He'd won an award from the ACLU."

Lucy walks over carrying a full trash bag. "I think I might have seen that show too. Didn't he also write for *Mad* magazine?"

I carefully flip through the brittle pages of the old magazine. "I think their offices were in the same building."

Jess wrinkles her nose. "My brother used to read *Mad* when he was a kid. My mother hated that magazine."

Marina hops out of the van. "Smart woman. I got so sick of my cousin saying 'What? Me worry?' like that creepy Alfred E. Newman who was always on the cover."

"Speaking of stupid, listen to this," I say after scanning a column called the Conspiracy Corner. "It says Adlai Stevenson didn't really die of a heart attack."

Mary Alice stands up, stretching her legs. "Don't tell me. He was murdered by the CIA."

"You're not far off. At least that's the case the author of the article is trying to make. He says it was because Stevenson was ready to tell the truth about Vietnam."

Did people really believe this stuff?

chapter TWELVE

DRIED FRUIT

1. Choose only blemish-free fruits that are ripe but not overly ripe.
2. Get the fruit ready by washing, pitting, and slicing it. Try to keep slices uniform so they will take the same amount of time to dry. (Note: smaller pieces will dry more quickly.)
3. To preserve the color of the fruit, dip in 2 tablespoons of ascorbic acid mixed with 1 quart of water—or lemon juice.
4. Fruit may be dried in the sun or in an oven.

   Sun Drying: works best in areas with low humidity and 90–100 degree heat. To dry, spread on a screen in a single layer. Leave in full sun 2–4 days. Turn over one time during the drying process. Be sure to bring the fruit inside in the evening to prevent dew from collecting on it.

   Oven Drying: Preheat oven to 145 degrees, propping door open with wooden spoon to allow steam to escape. Spread fruit on a cotton sheet or cheesecloth and place directly on oven rack. It usually takes 6–12 hours to complete the drying process.

5. When fruit is dry, transfer to a large bowl and place in a warm, dry spot. You will be able to tell the fruit is ready if it is dry but still pliable. Stir a couple of times a day for 10–14 days.
6. If you plan to store fruit for a long time, place in deep freeze for 24 hours to kill any insect eggs.
7. Store in an airtight container, such as a self-sealing bag or glass jar, in a cool, dry place.

HOMEMADE ROOT BEER

2 ounces sassafras root

1 ounce ginger root

1 ounce dandelion root

2 ounces wintergreen root

2 ounces juniper berries, crushed

4 gallons water, divided

5 pounds sugar

1 cake compressed yeast

Bottles with caps or corks

Instructions

1. Mix together roots and juniper berries in large pot. Add 2 gallons water and bring to a boil. Reduce heat and simmer 20 minutes. Strain through cheesecloth.
2. Add sugar and remaining 2 gallons water.
3. Cool until lukewarm—about the temperature of milk you'd give to a baby. Crumble yeast and stir into liquid.
4. Let mixture settle. Strain into bottles, filling to within an inch of the top. Cap bottles. (You can also use corks if you like— but be sure to cork tightly.)
5. Store bottles in a warm room for a few hours. Then move to a cool spot for long-term storage.
6. Serve cold.

Makes approximately 5 gallons.

August 8, 1968

MIAMI—Delegates at the Republican National Convention have chosen Richard Milhouse Nixon as their nominee for president of the United States. Nixon, who overcame challenges by Nelson Rockefeller of New York and Ronald Reagan of California, is expected to choose Spiro Agnew of Maryland as his running mate. Later this month Democrats will gather for their convention in Chicago to nominate their candidate.

●

"Did you read this?" Denny pointed to the article he was reading in the latest issue of *The Realist*. He and Ali were sitting on the hood of the broken-down Ford Fairlane abandoned at Avalon a few months earlier. Levi had dubbed it the "Guest Room" and used it for "sojourners" needing a place to crash.

Ali looked over and read aloud the headline plastered across the page. "'The Yippies Are Going to Chicago.' Looks like Abbie Hoffman and the boys have something up their sleeves."

Denny grabbed a handful of the Dried Fruit Ali had made and lay back on the hood of the car to continue reading. Arlo Guthrie's new song, "Alice's Restaurant," was playing on the car's radio.

Ali sang softly along with the chorus. "You can get anything you want at Alice's Restaurant. Walk right in—"

"Listen to this." Denny began to read the article aloud. "'The life of the American spirit is being torn asunder by the forces of violence, decay, and the napalm-cancer fiend.' That is so right on!"

"Um." Ali took a swig from the bottle of Homemade Root Beer. The women had brewed a batch from roots Natalie dug up in the woods.

As he read, Denny's frustration grew. Abbie and the Yippies were right. You couldn't trust the government. LBJ gave a big speech about limiting the war—

but he still had half a million troops in Vietnam. And thirty thousand soldiers were already dead, with hundreds more reported each week. Meanwhile the loudest voices for freedom—Medgar Evers, JFK, Dr. King, and Bobby Kennedy had all been murdered. Racism. Bigotry. Corruption. Repression. This couldn't go on.

Denny continued to read aloud, using his index finger to punctuate the words. "We are the delicate spores of the new fierceness that will change America. We will create our own reality. We are Free America! And we will not accept the false theater of the Death Convention."

Denny sat up next to his wife, handing her the magazine. "We have to go to Chicago, Al. It's like Eldridge Cleaver says, 'If you're not part of the solution, you're part of the problem.' We can't sit on our hands any longer."

Ali sighed and shook her head. "Denny, you know we can't go to Chicago. What would we do with Maya?"

Denny shrugged. "Take her with us."

"To a protest?" Ali asked incredulously. "You know it's too dangerous."

"Then we can leave Maya here with—"

"Who?" Ali narrowed her eyes and threw the magazine on the hood of car. "Willow?"

Denny's jaw tightened. So he got a little friendly with Willow once or twice. Why did Ali have to get so uptight about it? *She* was his old lady—not Willow.

"I'm beginning to think Joe's right," he said slowly. "You've got a lot of puritanical hang-ups."

Ali let out a sarcastic laugh. "So, now Joe's your guru? Give me a break."

Denny looked away. What had happened to the fire Ali used to have for The Dream? They were going to change the world. Make a difference. It was like she wanted to give up everything they believed in just because they had a kid. But he was not selling out this time. Too much was at stake.

Denny stared at Ali, muscles working in his jaw. "Have it your way, babe.

Don't go to Chicago with me. Stay here with Maya. I'll be back in a couple of weeks."

"There is no way I'm staying here alone, Denny."

Ali slid off the hood of the car and padded barefoot to sit next to Maya under a black walnut tree. The baby was sleeping peacefully on a blanket—smooth cheeks flushed with the afternoon heat. Ali brushed away a fly that had lighted on the child's chubby leg.

"You know what kind of people show up here. It's not safe. I was scared to death when you took off for Memphis last spring and those Hells Angels showed up looking for Bruno."

"Come on, Ali, you told me yourself nothing happened. Be reasonable—"

"I'm the only one who *is* being reasonable!"

"Why can't you see—"

Ali's voice softened. "Den, I know you want to have a say about what goes on at the convention. The peace platform is important to me, too. But, baby, we have a family now—and Maya has to come before anything else."

Why couldn't Ali see that he *was* putting Maya first? Did she want their child to grow up in a world with an oppressive government? If they didn't stand up for the oppressed, then they were no better than the oppressors. When did Ali lose sight of this?

At that moment, all Denny was sure of was a strong need to mellow out. He hopped down from the hood of the rusted Ford and began to walk toward the Dining Hall. Behind him, he heard Ali's determined voice.

"Denny, if you leave me and Maya to go to Chicago, don't expect to see us here when you get back."

●

*K*elly's piles are growing. Among other things, the Sell pile contains a rusty lava lamp, a worn copy of *How to Keep Your Volkswagen Alive* by

John Muir, and several boxes of old magazines and newspapers and a variety of political campaign memorabilia.

My favorite find is a poster from the 1968 presidential campaign picturing peace candidate Eugene McCarthy—his comb-over blowing haphazardly with The Winds of Change. I might have to bid when Jess puts it up on eBay.

The Save pile would be nonexistent if Marina hadn't rescued a box of eight-track tapes headed for the dumpster. She is now busy unscrewing the tape player and mounting rack from under the dash of the minibus. She claims it's just what she needs to trick out her vintage convertible.

The Scrapbook pile has a small box of photos—mostly of Mary Alice as a baby. I'm surprised at her blank look as she flips through the photos. Almost as if she's looking at the snapshots of strangers.

chapter THIRTEEN

CHICAGO DOG

8 all-beef wieners

8 poppy seed hot dog buns

Yellow ballpark mustard

Chopped cucumber

Chopped pepperoncini

Chopped onion

Chopped red-ripe tomato

Celery salt

Dill pickle spears

Instructions

1. Grill wieners over high heat 3–5 minutes until browned.

2. Toast buns in 375-degree oven or on the grill.

3. Place wieners on toasted buns. Top each with mustard.

4. Add generous spoons of cucumber, pepperoncini, onion, and tomato. Sprinkle with celery salt. Place a dill pickle spear on top.

Serves 8.

GRANOLA

2/3 cup butter

1 cup honey

1/2 teaspoon cinnamon (if desired)

1/4 cup sesame seeds

1/2 cup shelled sunflower seeds

1 cup chopped walnuts

1 cup whole almonds

1 1/2 cups bran

4 cups rolled oats

1 cup dried cranberries

Instructions

1. Melt butter in a Dutch oven. Mix in honey and cinnamon (if desired). Remove from heat.
2. Add seeds and nuts. Mix thoroughly.
3. Stir in bran, then rolled oats. Add more oats if mixture is too wet and sticky.
4. Spread mixture on a cookie sheet.
5. Bake at 350 degrees 45 minutes, stirring every 10 minutes and adding the dried cranberries after 30 minutes. Granola will be golden brown when done.
6. Allow to cool thoroughly and store in a sealed container or self-sealing bag.

Makes about 8 cups.

Saturday, August 24, 1968

CHICAGO—Marshal training sessions organized by the National Mobilization to End the War in Vietnam (MOBE) continued in Lincoln Park today in preparation for the opening of the Democratic National Convention at the International Amphitheatre on the city's South Side. Yesterday the Youth International Party, or Yippies, nominated a pig as their presidential candidate, prompting a fracas and several arrests. Mayor Richard Daley has vowed to keep protesters from the convention site, but some worry his infamous "shoot to kill" directive given to police during the riots following the assassination of Dr. Martin Luther King Jr. has created an incendiary situation.

●

Denny leaned against a tree in Chicago's Lincoln Park, swigging from a bottle of orange soda. He had just finished lunch—a hearty Chicago Dog he'd bought from a street vendor. He watched a group of flower children practicing karate on a field in the distance and another weaving through the crowd in a Snake Dance. Denny waved off a girl with frizzy red hair and a grubby toddler in a backpack who tried to pull him into the fray. It had been a long morning, preceded by an even longer night.

Denny had driven through the night, reaching the outskirts of Chicago as daylight painted the sky pink. He stayed awake by eating the Granola Ali had packed for the trip and listening to Johnny Rabbit on KXOK, a rock station broadcasting from St. Louis. Exhausted, both physically and emotionally, he pulled over in a residential area to sleep for a couple of hours in the back of Camille.

This morning he decided to take the train that local residents called "the el" into downtown Chicago instead of driving. Now sitting in Lincoln Park and watching a blue Ford Galaxy with a sticker on its rear bumper proclaiming We Support Mayor Daley and Our Chicago Police crawl along LaSalle Drive, he knew he'd made the right decision to keep Camille away from the protest. He figured a hippie van might not be welcome in Mayor Daley's empire. He would have loved to give the uptight geezer a lawn job with Camille, but she was his ride home. He wasn't taking any chances of not being back in time for Maya's first birthday next week.

Maya.

He had hoped the excitement of the day would chase away the memory of dropping his wife and daughter off at the bus station in St. Louis last night, but it still throbbed like an open wound. Once it was clear Denny had his mind made up about joining the antiwar protest in Chicago, Ali had announced that she and Maya were going to her parents' home in the northwest Missouri town of Rock Port. She asked Denny to drop her and the baby off at the Greyhound bus terminal in downtown St. Louis on his way to Chicago. He had done his best to talk her out of it, but she wasn't budging. He'd never seen such steely resolve.

●

"Al, you know we don't have the bread for a bus ticket."

Denny leaned back on a large floor pillow in the back of the van and watched as Maya stacked some blocks he had made for her while Ali packed. He'd never seen his wife like this before. Her demeanor was in sharp contrast to the mellow tune by the Rascals playing on the radio. Ali certainly wasn't "Groovin'." Her movements were stiff—almost robotic. Mouth was set in a firm line. Ice hardened her green eyes.

It was the eyes that really scared him. He leaned forward. "Ali, did you hear me? I said I barely have enough gas money to get Camille up to Chicago."

"Don't worry." Ali continued to stuff clothing and other belongings into a rucksack. "I've got the bus fare covered."

"Where'd you get the money?" Denny tickled his wife's nose with the end of her long, blond braid. "You been holdin' out on me, baby?"

Ali glanced up from the T-shirt she was folding to meet her husband's eyes. "My dad bought the ticket."

Denny dropped the braid. "When did you talk to your old man?"

A flash of anger lit Ali's eyes. "I *didn't* talk to him. Have you forgotten we don't have a phone out here? Or a toilet?"

Denny looked away. Nothing was ever good enough for Ali. Some Earth Mother this chick had turned out to be.

Ali took a deep breath. "In the birthday card my parents sent last spring, Dad wrote that the door is always open for us back in Rock Port. He said there's a ticket waiting for me at the Greyhound counter in St. Louis if I ever need it. He has one for you, too, Denny."

"So your old man thinks I'm some kind of charity case who can't take care of my family." Denny slammed the door of the van with his fist.

Jolted by the sound, Maya began to cry.

"Now look what you've done." Ali picked up the baby. "Denny, why can't you control yourself?"

He raked his fingers through his long hair. "I'm sorry, Ali. I didn't mean to upset the baby. But I want to know what you told your dad about us."

Ali put Maya back on the floor of the van. "You know things haven't been cool between us . . . ever since you and—"

"Al, you know that didn't mean anything."

A tear leaked from the corner of her eye as she folded a stack of cotton diapers. He instinctively reached out to catch it with his fingertip before it slid down her cheek.

"Come on, babe. I said I was sorry."

Ali didn't reply. Instead she stood and tugged open a wooden cupboard Denny had built in the van last summer and removed a stack of photos. She rifled through the pile, pulled out a few to shove in the sack, and put the rest back in the cabinet.

"You're not going to need all this stuff," Denny said. "I'll only be gone for two weeks. Probably less."

Ali tightened the straps on the rucksack. "I have to feed Maya now. The bus leaves from St. Louis at midnight, so we better take off after dinner."

"I really wish you could see where I'm coming from with all this. I can't turn my back on The Cause. Abbie says it's a revolution and—"

Ali cut him off. "Stop. I don't want to hear about Abbie . . . or his Revolution."

"But—"

Ali put up a hand. "Do you remember what you told me Che Guevara said about a revolutionary?"

"Not off the top off my head but—"

"Che said, 'The true revolutionary is guided by great feelings of love.'"

Ali bent and stroked Maya's cheek before carefully picking the baby up. Before climbing out of the van, she turned and added with a catch in her voice, "Think about who—or what—it is you love . . ."

●

Remembering the picture of Ali walking away with Maya in her arms, Denny felt a lump in his throat and what seemed like a fist squeezing his heart. He wondered if this was what soldiers through the ages experienced when leaving their families to go to war. *But when the cause is noble . . . the sacrifice is worth it,* he told himself. And what cause is nobler than ending the oppression of the United States government?

Denny drained the last of the orange soda from his bottle and pushed himself off the ground. He'd better get going. In an hour, Levi and Joe would be waiting for him at the entrance to the Fieldhouse. The War was about to begin.

●

*L*ook at all these political buttons." I removed several out of an old cake tin and read the slogans as I lined them up on top of a cardboard box.

"Peace Now!"

"Stop the War!"

"Make Love. Not War."

"All we are saying is give peace a chance."

"Isn't that a Beatles song?" asked Kelly.

Jess stands up. "My parents refused to allow any Beatles records in the house after John Lennon told a reporter that the Beatles were more popular than Jesus."

"He really said that?" Kelly seals up a trash bag with a twist tie.

"He tried to backpedal," says Jess, "and said something like, 'If apologizing will make you happy—then I'm sorry.' But the gist of it was he didn't think he'd said anything wrong."

Lucy grabbed the roll of tape and began to seal a box of magazines. "I always wondered why my parents were so down on the Beatles. I thought it was because of that 'bed-in for peace' thing where John and Yoko stayed in bed for a week. I remember them being on television every night talking about their opposition to the war."

"I still don't get what the big sacrifice was. I wouldn't mind staying in bed for a week." I scoop the buttons back into the tin and place it in the Sell pile. "But I'd hate to see what my house would look like after I came out of the bedroom. It certainly wouldn't be peaceful."

Jess ripped another bag off the roll. "I read in *USA Today* that John Lennon now has his own action figure."

I howl at the thought of the famous rock star stocked alongside the Teenage Mutant Ninja Turtles. "You're kidding!" I sputter, trying to control myself.

"It's true. From his so called New York years, and it even talks."

Marina steps out of the van. "What's he say? 'I'm more popular than Barbie'?"

chapter
FOURTEEN

BBQ RIBS

These ribs take 2 days to make, but they're worth the effort. You start by baking them in a slow oven, marinating with a rub overnight, then grilling with a homemade sauce.

4 pounds baby-back pork ribs

2 teaspoons minced garlic

1 tablespoon sugar

1 tablespoon paprika

2 teaspoons salt

2 teaspoons black pepper

2 teaspoons chili powder

2 teaspoons ground cumin

1/2 cup dark brown sugar

1/2 cup cider vinegar

1/2 cup ketchup

1/4 cup chili sauce

1/4 cup Worcestershire sauce

1 tablespoon lemon juice

1/4 cup chopped onion

1/2 teaspoon dry mustard

1 teaspoon minced garlic

Instructions

1. Rub ribs with 2 teaspoons garlic and place on rack in roasting pan.

2. Cover with foil and bake at 300 degrees 2 1/2 hours. Cool.

3. To make rub, mix together sugar, paprika, salt, pepper, chili powder, and ground cumin. Rub over ribs. Cover and put in refrigerator overnight.

4. In saucepan, mix brown sugar, cider vinegar, ketchup, chili sauce, Worcestershire sauce, lemon juice, onion, dry mustard, and minced garlic.

5. Cook over low heat (uncovered) for 1 hour, being careful not to burn.

6. Reserve small amount for basting; remainder is a dipping sauce.

7. Grill ribs 10–15 minutes over medium heat, brushing with sauce on both sides.

8. Be sure to save some extra sauce to serve on the side.

Serves 4–6.

GOURMET GRILLED CHEESE

4 tablespoons butter

4 teaspoons Dijon mustard

4 teaspoons crushed garlic

6 ounces fontina cheese, shredded

6 ounces mozzarella cheese, shredded

2 ounces Parmesan or asiago cheese, shredded

2 green onions, thinly sliced

8 slices sourdough bread, thick-sliced

Instructions

You can make these on an outdoor grill, indoor grill, or in a pan.

1. Toss the cheeses and green onions together.
2. Divide the cheese mixture on four slices of bread. Top each with another slice of bread.
3. Melt butter. Whisk in mustard and garlic. Brush top of each sandwich with garlic/mustard/butter sauce. Place facedown on grill. Then brush remaining sauce on the other side of each sandwich.
4. Grill 3–4 minutes on each side until bread is golden brown and cheese is melted.

Makes 4 sandwiches.

Sunday, August 25, 1968

CHICAGO—A concert and antiwar rally drew close to 5,000 young people to Lincoln Park today. Organized by the Yippies, the event was billed as the "Festival of Life" to contrast with what they term the Democratic Party's "Festival of Death," set to open tomorrow at the International Amphitheatre. Police fear outbreaks of violence due to reports of the Yippies purchasing large amounts of hair spray from Old Town area stores. Police say the expulsion of hairspray can be used as a flame thrower when lit. According to a spokesman for the City of Chicago, "It is common knowledge that Yippies have no use for hair spray or other cosmetics for personal use."

●

"A hippie lawn party. That's the way the newscaster on Denny's transistor radio described the gathering at Lincoln Park. Now that he was here, he had to agree.

Instead of a passionate antiwar rally, the crowd was laid-back. Flower children in bell-bottoms and fringe stretched out on Indian blankets. A folk singer played an acoustic guitar on a makeshift stage. Dogs chased Frisbees. Even a motorcycle club, their colors sewn on jackets and jeans with rawhide lacing, seemed to groove with the vibe of the friendly crowd.

This wasn't at all what Denny had expected when he came to Chicago. Where were the passionate speeches? The protest marches? The revolution?

Yesterday he had waited three hours for Levi and Joe before giving up. Tired and unfamiliar with the city, he headed back on the el to Camille and crashed. This afternoon, as he walked through the huge crowd, his hopes for hooking up with his friends began to fade.

"Hey man, how's it hangin'?"

Denny turned toward the source of the voice. A bearded man with an eight-inch ball of red fuzz circling his head was grinning at him with yellow teeth. Denny looked from side to side, not sure if the guy was talking to him.

"Denny, right?"

"Yeah."

"Far-out. I thought it was you, man. You live at that commune down in Missouri."

Denny peered at the man more closely. "That's right, but . . ."

The man offered his hand to Denny. "Kevin. I came in with Harley. We crashed at your place."

Denny shook his hand. "You're Harl's friend! Now I remember. Sorry, man. You look different."

"It's the 'fro." He patted his hair. "I decided to go au naturel. Makes me look more like an anarchist."

Denny laughed. "Yeah, you've got it goin' on, man."

●

Kevin told Denny he had been in Chicago for the last few weeks training for convention week with the National Mobilization Committee (MOBE) and Students for a Democratic Society, or the SDS, as the organization was referred to by organizers. "That fascist pig Daley is trying to close down the city and silence the voice of the people. But he won't get away with it."

"What'd he do?" asked Denny as he and Kevin walked down Wells Street in the Old Town section of Chicago. Kevin had offered to introduce him to some of his friends in the SDS.

"Daley wouldn't grant permits for any of our demonstrations. He even ordered the police to wrap barbed wire around the amphitheater to keep protesters away from the convention."

Denny stopped on the sidewalk. "No way, man! He can't do that, can he? What about the First Amendment—free speech?"

Kevin glanced over both shoulders as if checking to see if anyone other than Denny was within earshot. "Don't worry. We're not gonna let that stop us. That's where the marshals come in."

"What's goin' down?" Denny whispered.

"Be cool, man. You'll find out when the time is right. That is, if you want in."

●

"So, what do you think of the scene over at Lincoln Park?"

Denny watched across the table as the young man with long sideburns and a droopy mustache sucked the last bit of barbeque sauce from a pork rib. A headband embroidered with an obscenity kept his long, stringy hair out of his eyes.

Not sure if he was free to answer honestly, Denny glanced at Kevin. All he knew about the man was that his name was Rob, and Kevin knew him from the SDS. The three men were sitting around a scarred wooden table in the tiny apartment kitchen of another stranger—a girl named Kristin who was a law student at Northwestern University and a member of SDS.

Kevin nodded. "It's cool."

Denny raked his fingers through his shaggy hair. "I don't know, man. I mean, the convention opens tomorrow. And the delegates are already arriving at the Conrad Hilton, right?"

Rob began to lick the sauce from his hands—one finger at a time. "So?"

"So why is everybody sitting around like it's some big party? If we don't get our act together, Humphrey's going to end up the nominee. Then there will be four more years of the status quo in Vietnam."

Rob exchanged a glance with Kevin before answering. "The music is just to draw the crowds, man. The beautiful people like a good time. Just wait. Jerry and Abbie will get them riled up tonight."

"But isn't there an eleven o'clock curfew? People will be leaving."

"We'll keep the bands going so they won't want to leave," Rob answered coolly. "That's how you gather the tribes. Sex, drugs, and good old rock and roll."

Denny eyed Kevin. "But the cops—"

"What are the cops gonna do if ten thousand hippies decide they want to camp in the park?" Kevin laughed. "They can't arrest us all. There'll be so much chaos the pigs won't know which way to turn."

Rob smiled. "That's the beauty of it. The Establishment is going to start the revolution themselves. They'll provoke all the violence and end up smashing the city. And this time, the whole world will be watching on television."

Kevin flashed another big yellow grin. "Far-out, huh?"

Denny nodded slowly. He wasn't sure what to think. Wasn't it hypocritical to be chanting "Peace Now" while hoping the cops would start busting heads so they'd look bad on television?

And what about the protesters? It seemed like they were being set up by the leaders of the SDS. People could get hurt—maybe killed. The whole thing didn't feel right.

"So Denny, you're in, right? We need a few more marshals."

Before Denny could answer, Kristin walked into the room carrying a large Boston fern and set it on the counter next to the sink. She picked up a small brass atomizer from the windowsill and began to spray the leaves of the plant.

"Hey Kris, come on over. There're plenty of BBQ Ribs to go around." Rob pulled out a chair next to him.

"You know I don't eat meat," she answered, her long chestnut hair camouflaging her expression.

Rob laughed. "Well, you better get used to it, babe. The streets of Chicago are going to be chock-full of barbecued pork this week."

●

All that's left is this box of chemistry books." Kelly shoves the box across the floor with her foot.

"And don't forget the hibachi." I hold up the little cast-iron BBQ with a rusty grill, a silver coating of ash lining its belly.

"I had one of those in college," said Jess. "Our stove went out, so we used it to cook for a couple of weeks until the landlord had a new one installed."

I wrinkled my nose. "Barbecue for two weeks? That had to get old."

Jess smiled. "We were very creative. I remember making what my roommates called Gourmet Grilled Cheese on our little grill."

"Grilled cheese on a BBQ pit?" Kelly shook her head. "Now I've heard everything."

"Don't make fun, Kel. George Foreman probably started the same way."

I hold up the hibachi once more. "Mary Alice, save or toss?"

"Throw it in the dumpster with the rest of the stuff. Those outdated chemistry books too. If there's room."

I set the grill on top of the box of books.

"I told you guys none of this would be worth keeping," Mary Alice continues. "It's just a bunch of junk. I don't know why I agreed to have it shipped here. What a waste."

"Don't say that." Lucy puts her arm around Mary Alice's shoulder. "You have the photos and your mom's recipes—"

"A shoebox. That's the extent of my life to him. A few photos and—" Mary Alice straightens her shoulders. "Let's finish up here. I'm ready to go home."

I'm beginning to have second thoughts about our intervention. Maybe some things are better left in the past. Mary Alice has a wonderful husband, great kids, a beautiful home. Why did we insist on dredging all this up?

It's Lucy who speaks up. "Jesus once asked a man who had been sick for thirty-eight years if he wanted to be healed."

Mary Alice turned away, but to Lucy's credit, she didn't waver. I knew it was probably taking all she had to offer the same kind of tough love she'd experienced a few months ago as she worked through her grief.

"I know it's hard to hear, sweetie," Lucy continued, "but the way I see it, you have the same choice. To choose not to feel—and live in denial. Or choose to be healed. So which is it?"

chapter
FIFTEEN

POWER TO THE PEOPLE PITAS

2 pita bread

2 tomatoes, diced

1 avocado, sliced

1 can kidney beans, drained

1 cup shredded cheddar cheese

1 cup sliced mushrooms

1 cup bean sprouts

1/2 cup olive oil

2 tablespoons red wine vinegar

1/4 cup sunflower seeds

Salt and pepper to taste

Instructions

1. Slice pitas in half.
2. Mix remaining ingredients and put into pitas.

Makes 4 sandwiches.

Wednesday, August 28, 1968

CHICAGO—Tensions flared last night when police refused to allow antiwar activists to spend the night in Lincoln Park. Enraged protesters poured into Old Town, smashing windows, setting fires, and wreaking havoc in protest of what they feel is the city's efforts to silence them. Delegates to the Democratic National Convention are expected to choose their party's candidate today as Hippies, Yippies (aligned with Abbie Hoffman's Youth International Party), and other demonstrators promise a day of protest that Chicago will never forget.

●

"Our goal with the Snake Dance is to scatter the police so that it's more difficult for them to maintain control of the crowd."

Denny stood in a group of about thirty hippies on a baseball field at the south end in Lincoln Park. Even at 9:00 a.m., the air was hot and thick as he listened to a tall, skinny activist conduct the training session for new SDS marshals.

After the violence of the last two nights, when police refused to let antiwar protesters sleep in Lincoln Park, Denny's view of The Revolution changed dramatically. He had witnessed firsthand what he felt were Gestapo tactics by the police to silence the voice of the people. Sure, it was all done under the guise of maintaining order, but that was the claim of repressive regimes throughout history. He was now convinced that no normal political solution would resolve the mounting oppression of the government. And he was determined to do his part to create a new world order.

After all, wasn't it Ghandi who said, "You must be the change you want to see in the world"? Denny was committed to fight for change.

"Okay, listen up people," shouted the group leader. "Line up side by side in rows of six facing me and link arms. That's right—just like in square dancing during gym class."

Denny wiped sweat from his brow as he fell in line at the end of the second row behind a burly man who looked like he belonged on the defensive line of the Chicago Bears. He exchanged a smile with the petite, curly-headed girl next to him in hip-hugger jeans and granny glasses.

Denny raised his elbow to link arms with the girl. "You think he'll ask us to do an 'allemande left' or a 'do-si-do' next?"

She grinned up at him, the sun reflecting off her glasses.

The leader picked up a metal pole about eight feet long and two inches in diameter and held it horizontally before the people in the front row. "Take the pole with both hands. That's right—keep your arms linked. Now, the rest of you, grab the belt of the person in front of you with both hands."

As the group packed closer together, Denny was glad he had picked a spot on the end. Since downtown Chicago bordered Lake Michigan, he had expected a cool summer breeze rather than this wall of humidity. So much for the "Windy City."

"The trick is," the leader continued as he inspected the perimeter of the group, "to synchronize your steps so you stay as close together as possible without stepping on the heels of the person in front of you when we move. It helps to chant."

The group started off by jogging in place and chanting, "Peace Now! Peace Now!" When the leader felt they had the hang of it, he began to lead them forward in straight lines across the park. They progressed to wavy lines, turning left and right—and finally practiced moving faster or slower at his command.

After about fifteen minutes, Denny was wiped out by the combination of heat, humidity, and collective body odor. Many in the group smelled like they hadn't showered in days. He was grateful when the instructor told them to take a break. As they sat on the grass of the outfield, a girl in tight jeans and a bright yellow halter top passed out water in paper cups.

Still standing, the leader addressed the group. "I know this whole Snake Dance thing may seem a little weird to those of you who haven't tried it in a protest situation. But I've seen it work—and work well. People get charged up moving in the formation and start chanting and yelling. Before you know it, the cops have lost control."

The girl with the granny glasses sitting next to Denny cupped her hand over her mouth to whisper to him. "I heard this is what Japanese students used in 1960. The riots kept Eisenhower from visiting the country."

"Far-out."

The instructor motioned to the group of hippies lounging on the bleachers at the side of the field. "Before you split, get with your captains so you are cool with your assignments for the rally this afternoon in Grant Park."

Denny saw Kevin ambling toward him. He drained the last of his water, crushed the paper cup, and pushed himself up from the ground.

"Later," he said to the girl.

She grinned and flashed him the two-fingered signal known to kids everywhere. "Peace."

●

"You got the Snake down, man?" Kevin slapped Denny on the back.

"I guess so. But is this really gonna work?"

"At the MOBE they told us the Snake will break right through a police line and keep the cops from making arrests."

"That is if people don't start falling over their feet. Especially if they're loaded or trippin'."

"Just keep the chants going and you'll be fine."

Denny smiled and shook his head. "Whatever you say, man. You're the captain."

Kevin looked up. "Cool, here comes Bernie. Right on time."

Bernie was a tall, stocky woman, draped in a multicolored caftan and wearing leather sandals. The two men watched as she crossed LaSalle Drive with a large canvas tote slung across her shoulder. Kevin waved to her and pointed to a large sycamore tree where a half dozen other hippies Denny knew were from Kevin's "unit" were sitting in the shade. One of the girls was spreading out a colorful tie-dyed sheet while another took food from a covered basket.

Once the group was settled and Kevin had asked one of the women to keep an eye out for any "pigs with big ears," he explained where each marshal was to be stationed. "Since we don't know what the cops are going to do, everything needs to be a little fluid. Remember, the goal is to—"

"Drive the pigs crazy!" A grubby hippie with a pockmarked face sneered, showing two missing teeth. "I'd like to get a pig alone and beat the—"

Kevin gave the man a sharp look. "Cool it, Dwayne. We wanna provoke the pigs to violence. Not start banging heads ourselves."

Denny blew out a long breath. He was glad to see Kevin take control. Just like there were crazy cops, there were crazy hippies in the movement. He wasn't comfortable with some group of freaks offing a cop.

"Speaking of which . . ." Kevin smiled. "Bernie has a little surprise to make your job easier."

Bernie looked over both shoulders before she removed a little bundle tied in a red bandanna out of her bag. "Is it cool?" she asked Kevin.

"Go ahead, pass them out."

"Okay people, these are called guerilla nails," Bernie explained in a low tone and handed a bundle to each person.

Denny carefully untied the bandana and peeked inside. There were several clusters of nails, sharpened at both ends and soldered together in the center.

Bernie sniggered. "Just toss one of these under a pig's tire—and *pssssst*—it's flat as a pancake. He ain't going anywhere."

"What about the cops on foot?" asked a shy girl with greasy blond hair. "How do we slow them down?"

Kevin rested his elbows on his knees. "We're working on some stink bombs to get the whole place heaving. Rob went to Walgreens for this foul-smelling hair remover his mother used when he was a kid. The lady at the counter got suspicious 'cause he was screwing the tops off and sniffing all these bottles. He decided to split before she called the cops."

"Have you thought about using butyric acid?"

All eyes turned to Denny.

"It's a chemical that smells just like vomit. Nasty stuff."

"Far-out," said Kevin. "Can you get that at Walgreens?"

"I don't think so. But the lab at Mizzou got their chemicals from a place called Central Scientific. I remember the address on the label was from Chicago."

"Are you a chemistry major?" asked a girl with frizzy black hair and a severe face.

"Chemical engineering."

"Righteous." Kevin leaned forward. "Could you make stink bombs with this stuff?"

"It dissolves in water, so I don't see why not. That is, if we can get the stuff from the chemical supply. I have wheels—so can check it out."

Kevin slaps his knee. "Groovy. You make up the stink bombs and meet me behind the pop stand at Grant Park to do the handoff."

"How are we gonna set 'em off?" asked Bernie.

Kevin grins. "Don't worry. I'll line up some chicks to do the deed at just the right time. Chicks are good for that kind of stuff."

Denny glanced around the circle to see if any of the women looked offended. But none even seemed to notice Kevin's demeaning comment. Denny knew Ali wouldn't put up with that. Better she wasn't here.

"Denny, my boy, am I glad those burnout friends of yours never showed up. The Movement's been waiting for a soldier like you." Kevin grabbed one of the pita sandwiches the girls were passing out for lunch and held it up in the air. "Watch out, capitalist pigs! The times are a-changin'."

"Here you go, man." Denny handed the six-pack of green glass 7Up bottles to Kevin, who was waiting for him behind a concession stand in Grant Park. The historic park was across the street from the Conrad Hilton Hotel, where the candidates, the press, and most of the delegates were staying.

Kevin took the carton and slipped it into his backpack. "This is it?"

"It's all you need. Each bottle has enough stink to clear a quarter mile—or more."

A few hours earlier Denny had carefully pried the metal caps off each bottle, replaced the pop with water, and added three drops of the chemical. The hardest part had been recapping the bottles to make sure the liquid wouldn't leak. From past experience in the lab, he knew the stench would cling to anything—fabric, glass, metal—and last for weeks.

"Cool." Kevin nodded approvingly. "By the way, Rob said to tell you we're meeting at Kristin's in the morning. Or feel free to stop by tonight if you need a place to crash."

"Thanks, man."

Kevin flashed the peace signal. "Later."

Finally Denny felt he was doing something to make the politicians listen. He wasn't on the sidelines any longer. He was part of The Revolution—and it was a rush.

But that afternoon, Denny had felt a different kind of rush. A stab of fear when he'd showed up at Central Scientific to purchase butyric acid. One glance at his unkempt appearance and the middle-aged receptionist had called her supervisor. After showing three different types of identification, including his old student ID from Mizzou, Denny was allowed to buy a small vial of the chemical. But not without signing a receipt for the purchase.

Denny hesitated as the receptionist handed him the clipboard for his signature. *But why worry?* he told himself. There was nothing illegal about buying butyric acid. He was only making a stink bomb. No one would be hurt. He shook off his uneasiness and scribbled his name on the receipt.

Now in Grant Park, Denny stepped from behind the refreshment stand to see journalist and author Norman Mailer climbing to the platform. Surrounding the crowd of several thousand gathered at the band shell were more than six hundred Chicago police officers. Denny looked up to see Illinois National Guardsmen posted on the roof of the nearby Field Museum.

"We are at the beginning of a war that will continue for twenty years," declared the popular author and former editor of *The Village Voice*. "The march today will be just one battle in this war, and I wish I could join you. But I have a deadline to meet."

"Write, baby! Write, baby!" the crowd chanted.

"You are beautiful people!" Mailer raised his hands to acknowledge the crowd before handing the microphone back to activist David Dellinger.

As instructed by the MOBE, Denny was posted at the rear, between the crowd and the police, when news began to spread that the delegates in the amphitheater had voted down the peace plank. The tension and frustration building in the crowd of fifteen thousand antiwar protesters felt to Denny like the prelude to one of the powerful tornados Midwesterners fear. He could relate. A storm was raging in him, too.

Then the storm hit.

"Take it down! Take it down!" the crowd chanted as a young man began to lower the American flag flying near the band shell. Police moved in to arrest him but were pushed back by a shower of debris from the angry protesters.

More police surged forward and began to attack the crowd with nightsticks. Finding all other exits blocked, protesters fled the park by crossing the Jackson Street Bridge with police in pursuit.

Behind him, Denny heard the sickening squish of a nightstick making contact with soft brain issue as a protester went down. Shocked and terrified, Denny continued across the bridge, knowing he had no chance against a police force fueled by frustration and rage.

On Michigan Avenue, an angry mob surrounded a police car, trying to tip it over. Denny caught a glimpse of the horror on the young officer's face as the crowd chanted, "Kill the pigs! Kill the pigs!"

Then came the tear gas. The first wave scorched Denny's lungs and burrowed deep into his eyes. He covered his face with his hands and screamed at the searing pain.

It wasn't supposed to happen like this.

●

What do you mean it's my choice? I never had a choice in any of it! My mother chose to leave my dad. And my dad chose to stay away—attached to his precious Cause."

I've never seen Mary Alice so angry. Or so animated by anything other than housework or crafts. She's pacing like a caged tigress.

"None of you know what it's like to have your *own father*—someone who is supposed to love you unconditionally—make a conscious choice to toss you aside like you didn't even exist. To choose this"—Mary Alice snatches from a box a copy of a Chicago newspaper with the headline "The Battle of Michigan Avenue" screaming across the front and shakes it in the air—"over you."

Mary Alice drops the paper on top of the stack and sinks down onto a sealed box. "He was supposed to be there. To protect me. To read to me at night. To help me with math. To teach me to drive. To walk me down the aisle at my wedding.

"He was supposed to love me. I was his daughter."

chapter
SIXTEEN

CHINESE BIRTHDAY NOODLES

1/2 pound Chinese noodles

1 tablespoon sesame oil

1/2 pound fresh spinach

1 cup vegetable stock (or chicken broth)

1 tablespoon soy sauce

1/2 teaspoon cornstarch (dissolved in 1 teaspoon water)

1/2 teaspoon salt (optional)

6 eggs

2 tablespoons chopped chives

Instructions

1. Add noodles to 4 quarts boiling water. Cook 2–3 minutes until tender. Drain. Place in large, wide bowl or 6 individual bowls. Mix in sesame oil and set aside.
2. In wok or large frying pan, bring 2 tablespoons water to a boil. Add spinach. Cook 1 minute. Drain, squeeze out excess water. Chop. Put on top of noodles in bowl or individual bowls.
3. Combine vegetable stock or chicken broth, soy sauce, cornstarch mixture, and salt (if desired) in a small saucepan. Bring to a boil. Mixture will thicken. Reduce heat to keep warm.
4. In wok or deep frying pan, bring 4 cups water to a boil. Break each egg into a small dish one at a time and slip into boiling water. Turn down heat and cook 2 minutes.
5. When eggs are cooked, put on top of noodles/spinach. Add the hot broth to the bowl or bowls. Sprinkle with chives. Enjoy!

Serves 6.

crime & clutter

Thursday August 29, 1968

CHICAGO—An undetermined number of antiwar demonstrators sustained injuries yesterday in what some are calling a police riot at the intersection of Balboa and Michigan Avenue. Teams from the Medical Committee for Human Rights estimate that volunteers treated more than a thousand demonstrators, bystanders, and reporters who were severely beaten by the police. Fumes from the tear gas used by the police and stink bombs thrown by the protesters drifted into nearby hotels and buildings, causing evacuations that added to the mass confusion. The arrest count for convention week disturbances now stands at 668.

●

"It's the birth of The Revolution, people!" Kristin walked into the room carrying a large earthenware bowl of skinny Chinese Birthday Noodles. She set it on the round cable spool used as a coffee table.

Rob scooted away from the group of six young men and women huddled around the small black-and-white television set and dished up a plate of noodles using the chopsticks Kristin had placed in the bowl.

"After what went down last night, the government has lost its credibility in the eyes of the American people," he said, piling his plate high.

Exhausted, but too keyed up to sleep, Denny couldn't tear his eyes from the flickering images on the television screen. A network anchorman was soberly providing a voice-over to the horrific footage of the riot from the previous evening . . .

The scenes you are watching occurred last night in front of the Conrad Hilton Hotel in Chicago, where thousands of Americans, both young and old, witnessed an explosion of raw, brutal, sadistic police force that marks one of the darkest hours of any police department in the country. Over and over again, the police charged into the thickly packed demonstrators, many who could not flee because they were trapped. They would try to run one way and the police would charge from another direction and catch them in the middle. Many of the demonstrators, as you can see, were dragged along the asphalt road by their feet by a policeman while another beat them with his nightstick . . .

Denny turned away from the television, shuddering as the nightmare of the previous evening washed over him. Luckily, the effects of the tear gas wore off quickly, and he was able to break free of the riot and find his way back to Kristin's apartment in Old Town. After a cold shower to remove the last vestiges of the chemical from his body and clothing, he spent the night ushering in a steady stream of SDS marshals seeking a place to crash.

"Did you hear what that buffoon Daley said at his press conference this morning?" asked a young man who was still wearing a black armband from the night before.

"What'd he say?" asked a young woman in a wrinkled peasant blouse and blue jeans. Stretched out on the floor, she rolled over and propped her head on an elbow.

"Get this. Daley said, 'The policeman isn't there to create disorder. The policeman is there to preserve disorder.'"

Derisive laughter skittered around the tiny living room.

"They did a great job last night," said Rob despite a mouthful of noodles. "Maybe Daley should give them all a medal."

More laughter.

"Speaking of medals, I think our man Denny here deserves one." Kevin slapped Denny on the back. "You should have seen the pigs heavin' after we dropped a couple of Denny's stink bombs. Good work, man."

Rob nodded as he took a second helping of noodles. "I've been thinking The Movement could use a mad scientist like you, Denny. I mean, we could make our own tear gas to turn on the pigs. Or mix up a nice Molotov cocktail."

"Far-out," said Dwayne, a ghoulish smile lighting up his scarred face. "That'd make 'em squeal all right."

Denny looked back at the violent images—the rampage of the Chicago police—playing on the screen. Maybe Rob was right. It sure looked like a non-violent revolution was impossible.

As if reading his mind, Kristin spoke up. "The gun in The Establishment's hand makes them secure in their exploitation. To defend ourselves against mounting pig terror, we must take up arms."

A chorus of "right ons" bounced around the room.

Kristin stood and walked to the window, her body silhouetted in the morning sunlight. "An armed People's Militia can provide collective self-defense for our homes, our gatherings, our land, and our lives. We will take over the cities one at a time. Just like the National Liberation Front is doing in Vietnam.

"Then we'll be able to create a society that is free and joyous," she continued. "Where everyone is fed and educated. And everyone has a chance to express themselves artistically, politically, and spiritually."

The room exploded in affirmation. "Far-out."

As Kristin spoke, Denny closed his eyes to picture the kind of society he wanted to help build for Ali and Maya.

Just. Equal. Free.

Denny started to drift off.

Bam! The door to the apartment was kicked open.

"FBI! Don't move!" a voice boomed. "You are all under arrest."

The last thing Denny heard before the snap of handcuffs on his wrists was Rob choking on a noodle.

●

The mood is subdued as we load the last of the boxes into Jess's SUV. We are all aware of Mary Alice's raw emotions. Except for one small box, she has decided to sell the rest of her dad's things—including the minibus. Jess volunteered to drop everything off at a nearby shop that will list, sell, and ship your stuff on eBay for a percentage of the cost. M.A. plans to donate the proceeds to Lucy's shelter.

Jess, Lucy, and Mary Alice are already standing, ready to go, by the Suburban. M.A. says she just wants to forget about her dad and move on.

Maybe she's right. After all, what do I know? I have no idea what it's like to have your father abandon you.

Even Marina, with all her bravado, suffered tremendously when her husband left her. It took her several years before she could trust a man again—and she still sometimes keeps Jeff at arm's length even though he's been nothing but devoted to her. And poor Lucy, who lost both her husband and her mom in the space of a year. Lucy and Marina, at least, understand loss and abandonment.

But not to ever experience the special bond that exists between a father and child must be devastating. Who are we to tell M.A. it's her choice to heal? None of this was her fault. She should be able to handle it in her own way without a cadre of female Dr. Phils telling her she has to deal with her "issues."

Right then and there I make a decision. I will pray for my friend, but I will keep my opinions to myself. No more amateur advice.

"What's that in your back pocket, Liz?"

I feel behind me and pull out a fat manila envelope. "I forgot all about this. I found it when I was cleaning out the glove box."

"Well, let's see what's in it," Kelly demands.

I hand the envelope to her.

Marina slams the door of the van. "I gave the old girl the once-over."

She pats the side of the old minibus appreciatively. "And it looks like we're good to go. You ready to button things up?"

"We may have a little problem." Kelly holds up a packet of handwritten letters tied with a pink ribbon. "These are addressed to 'Maya.'"

"From her dad?" asks Marina.

"Looks like it."

Marina moves closer. "What do they say?"

Kelly gasps. "Mary Alice is standing right over there. I'm not opening her letters! I think it's illegal anyway."

"Nope. The law only applies if the letter is delivered by the post office."

"It's the same principle, Marina," Kelly huffs.

Marina glances at Jess, Lucy, and Mary Alice standing by the car. "What if she wasn't looking? Would you read them then?"

Now it's my turn to gasp. "Marina! That's despicable."

"That's what you say, Lizzie." Marina raises her eyebrows. "But I *know* what you'd do."

"Will you two quit acting like you're in grammar school?" Kelly hisses.

I knew it. Kelly saw the staring contest. Why do I let Marina do this to me?

M.A. peeks in the door. "Are you girls ready to go yet? It's starting to get dark."

The three of us exchange glances like we've been caught with our fingers in a cheesecake. Or a cannoli.

Kelly holds up the packet of letters, tied in a neat little bow with the faded pink ribbon. "Liz found these in the glove compartment earlier and forgot to give them to you."

I feel my face getting hot. *Why did Kelly have to add that little detail?*

Mary Alice takes a step closer. "What is it? More political pamphlets? Goodness, for making so much noise about saving the environment, these people sure wasted a lot of paper." Her attempt at levity doesn't quite reach her eyes.

Kelly hands the letters over. "They're addressed to you. I suspect they're from your dad."

Jess walks into the storage unit with Lucy in tow. "What's going on? I thought we were ready to take off."

"We may need just a few more minutes—" I begin.

"Nope. I'm ready to go." Mary Alice's voice is hoarse as she flips through one end of the stack without untying the ribbon. "Just let me toss this in the dumpster."

Kelly grabs Mary Alice's arm. "No, M.A.! You need to at least—"

Mary Alice gently twists away from Kelly's grasp. "I've tried to be patient with you all because I know you are only doing what you think is best. But enough is enough. I am not a child and would appreciate it if you would allow me to handle this in my own way."

The five of us watch in stunned silence as our mild-mannered friend turns on her heel and lobs the packet of letters in a perfect arc into the open dumpster. "Three points. Let's go."

CHAPTER
SEVENTEEN

JOSH'S CHEESEBURGER PIE

1 pound ground beef

1/2 cup chopped onion

1 teaspoon minced garlic

1/3 cup ketchup

2 tablespoons mustard

1/4 teaspoon salt

1/8 teaspoon ground pepper

1 (16 ounce) can corn, drained

1 (4 ounce) can diced green chilies, drained

2 cans refrigerated crescent rolls

1 cup shredded cheddar cheese

1 cup French's French Fried Onions (optional)

2 eggs, beaten

1 egg yolk, beaten

1 tablespoon water

Instructions

1. Brown beef with onion and garlic. Drain.

2. Stir in ketchup, mustard, salt, pepper, corn, and chiles.

3. On floured surface, unroll dough from 1 can of crescent rolls. Press together perforations, and roll dough to about 12-inch diameter. Press into pie plate.

4. Spoon meat mixture into dish. Sprinkle with cheese and spread fried onions on top if you are using them. Pour 2 beaten eggs over top.

5. Unroll dough from second can of crescent rolls. Press together perforations, and roll out to an 11-inch diameter.

Place on top of pie. Trim and pinch together with bottom dough layer.

6. Combine egg yolk and water. Brush over top of dough.
7. Bake at 350 degrees about 40 minutes or until nicely browned.

Serves 8 (or 4 hungry teenage boys).

S'MORES À LA JOSH

6 cups miniature marshmallows

1/3 cup corn syrup

6 tablespoons butter

1 teaspoon vanilla

7 cups graham cereal

2 cups semisweet chocolate chips

Instructions

1. In large microwave-safe bowl, melt 5 cups marshmallows, corn syrup, and butter. Stir in vanilla.
2. Add cereal, chocolate chips, and remaining cup of marshmallows. Stir until coated.
3. Press into greased 9x13-inch pan. When cool, cut into bars.

*I*t doesn't take much to melt a mom's heart. All a kid needs to do is offer a kind word or thoughtful gesture. Toss in a warm hug, and most moms become a puddle of goo. Tonight is one of those nights.

My heart begins to warm as soon as I walk in the front door after Jess drops me off. The house smells wonderful.

That can't be dinner in the oven, could it? I must be in the wrong house.

Or . . . maybe John is paying me back for making him breakfast in bed this morning.

Frankly, I doubt it. He pretty much used up his "sensitivity allotment" for the week when he came home early last night to help with FAC. As sweet as he is, he's still a *guy*. And it's not my birthday.

I follow my nose to the kitchen. Josh is standing behind the center island with a big, metal-mouthed smile. Ketchup smeared on his oversized white T-shirt and a bit of chocolate on his upper lip. Adorable.

"Joshie?" With my heart quickly turning to mush, I revert to his "baby" name. He doesn't seem to notice. "Did *you* cook dinner?"

"Yeah," he says, brown eyes sparkling. "I knew you'd be tired after working all afternoon."

He knew I'd be tired. My sixteen-year-old son knew I'd be tired. So he made dinner. Go ahead, Josh, ask me for anything. An unlimited cell-phone plan. A new car. Your own apartment. Our life savings. I won't be able to deny you anything.

Luckily, I keep these thoughts to myself. "You made dinner? By yourself?" I manage to choke out.

"Cheeseburger Pie and those S'mores bars from Christmas."

"Cheeseburger Pie? How in the world did you know how to make—"

Josh grins. "I got the recipe off the Internet."

Not worrying a bit about the transfer of ketchup stains, I draw my little guy—who happens to be almost six feet tall—into my arms for a hug. "I am so proud of you. Thank you, sweetie."

"Mom, it isn't that big of a deal." Josh pats me on the head and pushes out of my embrace. "I just wanted to help out. You helped me with my psych experiment yesterday."

So when has that ever mattered?

Like scores of mothers before me, I've gotten used to having a "thankless job." It is supposed to be my privilege to be chauffeur, chef, tutor, laundress, housekeeper—and, when required, guinea pig. I didn't think my children even noticed what I did for them. Except perhaps on Mother's Day, when they are required by social custom to acknowledge the "selfless acts of dear old mum."

Not about to let these thoughts ruin the moment, I squeeze Josh's shoulder. "Well, at the very least, let me set the table. I can't wait to try that Cheeseburger Pie. It smells heavenly."

Josh graces me with another metal-mouthed smile, basking in his culinary accomplishment. "I guess it turned out okay."

At that instant, it dawns on me. An epiphany. A lightbulb moment. The true reward of this "thankless job" comes when a mom looks at her children and thinks, *They are good people.*

In spite of my mistakes.

This is one of those times.

Now it's *my* turn to say thanks. To God for allowing me to have this wonderful, thankless job.

●

"This is good, Josh." John takes another slice of the now infamous Cheeseburger Pie.

I agree. "It's delicious."

I have to be careful not to make too much of Josh's thoughtfulness.

I've learned that overcomplimenting one child can spark a bad case of sibling rivalry. One would think such praise would prompt siblings to try to outdo each other to please their parents. But it's usually the opposite. If one child interprets a sibling's good deed as "sucking up," the "good" child will go out of his or her way to prove this is not the case.

Parents must walk a thin line to maintain household equilibrium. Not an easy task. One wrong move and the cycle of sibling rivalry starts spinning out of control. Tonight the first sign that trouble may be brewing comes from Katie.

"Is this hamburger from a cow that was raised on a Christian ranch?"

I almost choke on my food. "What?" I ask, coughing.

Hannah, who is sitting next to me at the table, pounds me on the back. "Are you all right, Mom?" she asks as she tries to dislodge the mystery substance I've sucked into my windpipe. "Katie just wants to know if the cow was a Christian."

This clarification causes me further respiratory distress. I notice John trying to clear his throat too.

Josh snorts. "Cows can't be Christians, bubble brain. It's in the Ten Commandments."

John wipes his mouth with his napkin. "Actually, Josh, that's not true. The Ten Commandments don't say anything about—"

"Then are Uncle Tom's cows Christians?" interrupts Hannah.

"Hannah, what I'm trying to explain—"

Hannah looks like she is ready to cry. "So Uncle Tom's cows aren't going to heaven? What about dogs? Is Daisy going to heaven?"

Josh can't bear to see his little sister upset. "Of course dogs go to heaven," he says in a soothing tone. "Remember we watched the movie together?"

Hannah smiles adoringly at her big brother. I don't have the heart to tell her that the Bible doesn't specifically address the eternal destiny of animals. Apparently neither does John.

"Just to clarify," John tries, "the Ten Commandments do not mention cows—or any animal for that matter."

"I wasn't asking if the cow was Christian." Katie looks pointedly at Josh. "We were discussing a new trend at school yesterday called 'clanning,'" she explains. "Faith Popcorn—the trends lady—says faith-friendly foods are the latest thing. I was just wondering if this meat came from a Christian ranch." She smiles. "That's all."

From where I'm sitting, it looks like sibling rivalry is going to be the least of our problems.

●

"Well, that wasn't as bad as I expected." John switches on the dishwasher after we've cleaned up the kitchen from dinner.

It takes me several seconds to realize he is referring to the shape of the kitchen—not our dinner conversation. "I have to admit. Josh is a much neater cook than I am. Do you think he has my mom's neat gene?"

Hannah interrupts before John can answer. Probably a good thing. Even though I'm the one who made the disparaging comment about my housekeeping ability, no wife wants her husband to agree.

Hannah's blue eyes plead with me. "Mom, will you take me and Kimberly to the mall?"

John comes to my rescue before I have a chance to answer. "Hannah, I just took you to the mall last night. Your mom's had a long day and she's tired."

I smile gratefully at John and turn back to Hannah. "Sweetie, I normally would be happy to take you but—"

"No, you wouldn't," she retorts.

"Excuse me?"

"Mom, you are *never* happy to take me to the mall. You always have some excuse for not taking me."

"Hannah, that's not true—"

Hannah sinks into a chair at the kitchen table. "I so need a personal assistant."

John laughs. "A personal assistant?"

"Why are you laughing, Dad?"

"*I've* never thought about getting a personal assistant. And I'm forty-four years old."

"Are you kidding? I've wanted a personal assistant since I've been, like, ten."

"But you're only eleven now."

Noting my husband's frustration, I wink in an effort to communicate that we'll laugh about this later. "So what would your personal assistant do, Hannah?" I ask.

Hannah grabs one of the S'mores bars left over from dessert and places it on a napkin in front of her. "Mainly drive me around without complaining. Take me shopping whenever I want. And, of course, give me money if I get low."

I notice John's ears are starting to get red as he wraps a dishtowel tightly around his hand. "Kind of like your mom and I do now?"

Hannah arches an eyebrow. "No. She'd be nice about it. And she'd have a nice car."

Oh.

"She would also let me have all the pets I want. And she would take care of them. I would have a big aquarium with all these fish, and she would change the water." Hannah looks in my direction. "Without making a big deal about it."

Hannah has a point here. It amazes me that children who can rattle off the names of the musicians in Switchfoot can't remember how to change the water in the goldfish bowl. I've tried to be "firm" as John says and just refuse to do it. But it breaks my heart to see poor Andy swimming around in that murky water. And my kids know it. They also know the poor dog would starve if it wasn't for me. I've always wondered how "good" parents navigate these moral dilemmas. I can't imagine Carol Brady letting a goldfish die because Peter keeps forgetting to change the water. But then, she did have Alice to clean the bathrooms and do all the cooking.

No time to think about this now. Hannah is on a roll. A dreamy look envelops her face as she continues describing her ideal personal assistant. "And how great would it be to have someone pack for me when I travel?"

This is getting good. I sit down at the table. "So are you planning any trips in the near future?"

Hannah daintily wipes chocolate from the corner of her mouth. "I *would* if I had a personal assistant. She could make the airplane reservations. And line up a cool hotel room. The kind that has a minifridge."

John leaves the room. Hannah's last comment must have been too much for him. After all, the poor man can only take so much. He's probably still fuming about the kids raiding the minifridge one of the few times we stayed at a full-service hotel on vacation—adding sixty-two dollars to our bill. He still thinks a law should be passed preventing anyone from charging four dollars for a Snickers bar.

Now, if John had a personal assistant, she could get right on that.

chapter
EIGHTEEN

EASY CHICKEN SOUP

6 meaty chicken pieces (breasts or thighs, skin removed)

1 cup chopped onion

1 teaspoon chopped garlic

1 cup sliced celery

3 carrots, chopped or sliced

8 cups water

2 bouillon cubes (crushed)

1 package frozen egg noodles

1/2 cup chopped fresh parsley

Salt and pepper to taste

Instructions

1. Brown chicken, onion, garlic, celery, and carrots in oil.
2. Add water and cook until chicken is no longer pink—about 45 minutes.
3. Remove chicken pieces from broth. Remove meat from bones when cool. Cut into bite-sized pieces.
4. Add noodles to simmering broth and cook until tender—usually 20 minutes.
5. Add chicken and parsley. Season with salt and pepper to taste.
6. Heat, serve, and get well soon!

Serves 6–8.

CRANBERRY TEA (AKA THE CURE)

1 (16 ounce) package fresh cranberries

8 cups water

2 cups orange juice (fresh is best)

Juice of two lemons

2 cinnamon sticks

1 teaspoon whole cloves

3/4 cup sugar

Instructions

1. Wash cranberries.

2. Add to water and boil until cranberries pop.

3. Add remaining ingredients and let steep at least 30 minutes.

4. Strain and serve warm.

Makes about 12 cups or 8 (12 ounce) servings.

MOM'S BRAN MUFFINS

The batter for these scrumptious muffins can be made ahead and kept tightly covered in the refrigerator for up to 2 weeks. Then you can easily bake fresh muffins each morning.

2 1/2 cups buttermilk (or replace 1/4 milk with 1/4 cup vinegar)

1/2 cup vegetable oil

2 eggs

3 cups raisin bran cereal

2 1/2 cups flour

1 cup sugar

1 1/4 teaspoons baking powder

1 teaspoon baking soda

1 teaspoon salt

1/2 cup chopped nuts

Instructions

1. Mix buttermilk, oil, and eggs thoroughly in a large bowl.
2. Add remaining ingredients. Mix until dry ingredients are moistened. Do not overmix.
3. To bake, fill greased muffin cups half full (or use paper muffin cups). Bake 20–25 minutes at 400 degrees until a toothpick inserted in the center comes out clean.

Makes 30 muffins.

$\mathcal{J}$ohn is home sick today with what he insists is the flu. Although I've tried to explain that his symptoms point to a spring cold rather than the flu, he is in no mood to listen.

Waving for me to hand him the box of antiviral tissues, my ailing hubby explains his reasoning in a nasal voice. "Liz, just because I got a flu shot doesn't mean I can't get the flu. There are hundreds of different strains of viruses going around each year. Who knows what's attacking my immune system?" He blows his nose and holds the used tissue in my direction. "What should I do with this?"

Goodness!

Men can be such babies when they're sick. This isn't just my opinion. I have research to back it up. I was reading the other day about a study done by a pharmaceutical company that found one in three men took time off work because of a cold or flu, compared to only one in five women. This is definitely not a surprise to mothers who carefully save all their sick days so they can be available to take care of other family members.

Marina says if men had to go through labor, the human species would be extinct by now. She may be right.

That said, I have to admit a certain pleasure at being able to pamper John when he's under the weather. It's my way of thanking him for all the times he gets the car and picks me up at the door on a cold day. Or opens a jar of pickles with an impossibly tight lid. Or pumps gas at the station while I sit in the car. And carries my suitcase in the airport. I enjoy the role of "helpless" woman when it's to my advantage, so it's only fair that he have the chance to act helpless every once in a while.

After getting John a wastebasket to keep near his chair for used tissues, a cup of my special Cranberry Tea, and the remote for the television, I head to the kitchen to check on the pot of chicken soup I put on this morning. Mothers throughout time have known this savory broth is a natural cure and feel vindicated by recent studies that show Mother really does know best.

My nose tells me the soup is ready, so I dish out two bowls and decide to join John in the family room. "Think you can eat a little soup, sweetheart? It will help your cold. I mean . . . flu."

"I guess I better try to eat something."

I put the tray across his lap. "Researchers say chicken soup boosts your immune system. I even heard that the protein released when you cook the chicken is similar to a prescription drug for bronchitis?"

John tucks the napkin under his chin. "Interesting."

"And the garlic and pepper work like a cough medicine to thin mucus."

"I've always wanted thin mucus." John grins and picks up his spoon. "You've really read up on this, haven't you?"

"Of course. Do you think I'd go to all the trouble to make homemade soup if it's not going to do any good? If that were the case, I might as well give you a bag of chips and a box of cupcakes."

"That's my Lizzie. Always thinking." John takes a spoonful of soup.

I glance at the television and notice he has it tuned to an episode of *Pimp My Ride*. The crew of gearheads is installing a big-screen television with a satellite-dish hookup in an SUV. I have visions of my husband and son holed up in our minivan on Saturdays, watching an endless stream of sporting events.

I decide to take action before he gets any ideas. "Do you mind if we watch something else?"

John starts flipping through the channels with the remote. "What do you want to watch?"

"Let's see what's on. I don't usually watch television during the day." I take every opportunity I can to dispel the myth that a stay-at-home mom spends all day watching television and eating bonbons.

John stops on the A&E channel. "How about this?"

"*Dog the Bounty Hunter.* I don't think so."

John continues with a man's favorite activity. Channel surfing.

"This looks good," I say as he lands on the Do It Yourself network. I've always wanted to check out *The Queen of Clean.*

"Come on, Liz. This looks—"

"I might get an idea for my column. Just for a few minutes." I flash my best puppy-dog pout. "And then I'll watch a few minutes of *Dog* with you."

John sets the remote on the arm of his chair. The universal sign of surrender among the male species. "Since when have you been interested in a show about cleaning? Are you trying to keep up with Mary Alice?"

"I'll never be able to keep up with Mary Alice. Just like you'll never get around to 'pimping your ride.'"

John scowls. "Is that a dare?"

I laugh. "Definitely not. Now shhh! I'm missing the Queen's address to her adoring subjects."

●

I've never been so happy to be interrupted by a phone call. *The Queen of Clean* has spent the last ten minutes helping a triathlete remove grease stains from her bike shorts. When I see the episode is focusing on my two least favorite subjects—laundry and exercise—I suggest switching back to see what notorious criminals Dog was trying to apprehend. But John won't hear of it.

"Let's see what she has to say. You never know when you'll need to get stains out of your bike shorts. Maybe this year you'll decide to join Marina on the BRAN."

I glare at him. The Bike Ride Across Nebraska, or BRAN as it is affectionately referred to by the hundreds of participants who know the difference between a toe clip and platform, is Marina's pet project. For the last six or seven years, she's been trying to convince FAC to enter as a team.

Fat chance. And *fat* is the operative word.

There is no way I am going to spend a week perched on one of those skinny bicycle seats, riding across the state of Nebraska during the day and sleeping in a tent at night. The last time I hopped on a bicycle was when I tried a spinning class at the gym. After that experience, I vowed never to mount that beast again . . .

*O*kay people, on your bikes! Today we're heading to the White Mountains of New Hampshire!"

My expedition into the world of "spinning" is not starting out well. The lean instructor with her muscular legs and short haircut reminds me of the sadistic gym teacher I had in junior high—Ms. Payne. I had a sneaking feeling this class might bring back memories I had successfully repressed for thirty years.

After adjusting the height of the seat, I climb aboard one of the stationary bikes lined up in front of a mirror spanning the wall in the front of the exercise room. I know this mirror is supposed to help determine if you are doing an exercise correctly, but every woman I know avoids looking at it at all costs. In my opinion, mirrors are just another sadistic tool of the exercise industry to keep you sweating.

Averting my gaze from the mirror, I tried to find a comfortable position on the bicycle seat. The skinny seat feels like I'm sitting on a branch. I determine I must be doing something wrong.

To avoid injuring myself, I decide to ask our "spinning coach" for help. After all, that's why I am paying a membership fee. "Umm . . . this is my first time taking the class and—"

The instructor is already pedaling at a good clip. "Just pedal. It's not rocket science, is it, class?"

Nervous laughter skitters across the room from the dozen or so other riders already fastened into their toe clips and heading up the first hill of our trek to view the blazing colors of fall.

Did Ms. Payne have a wicked younger sister?

I press on in a shaky voice. "I was just wondering if all the seats are the same size. This one seems—"

"You gotta toughen up those glutes, soldier."

Soldier? I thought we were touring the White Mountains. Not slogging through boot camp. Tour guides are supposed to be soft and bubbly, laden with tasty snacks for weary travelers. This woman is a drill sergeant from my worst military nightmare.

Not wanting to appear a wimp, I *soldier* along while enduring the most excruciating pain since my last episiotomy and vowing to cross New Hampshire off my "to see before I die" list. By the time we reach the crest of the third "mountain," I've had enough.

I extricate myself from the tortuous bike and mop my sweaty brow. "I've decided to take the tram. . . ."

●

*N*ope. There is nothing that will convince me to participate in the BRAN—including a life supply of my Mom's delicious Bran Muffins.

But John, watching smugly while the Queen of Clean spiffs up a pair of bike shorts, doesn't need to know this. At least not now. I need to answer the telephone.

The caller ID says it is Mary Alice.

chapter NINETEEN

CINNAMON DREAM MOCHA

8 cups water

4 heaping scoops ground coffee

2 cinnamon sticks, broken

1 teaspoon whole cloves

brown sugar (to taste)

half-and-half (to taste)

Instructions

1. Fill coffeemaker with 8 cups water.

2. In filter basket, put coffee, cinnamon sticks, and cloves.

3. When coffee is brewed, sweeten to taste with brown sugar and half-and-half.

Makes about 9 cups or 5–6 (12 ounce) servings.

APPLE ALMOND BISCOTTI

1 cup sugar

1 cup packed brown sugar

1/4 cup vegetable oil

2 eggs

1/3 cup sour cream

1 tablespoon apple cider

1/3 cup slivered almonds

2 1/2 cups flour

2 teaspoons baking powder

2 teaspoons ground cinnamon

1/2 teaspoon ground cloves

1/4 teaspoon ground ginger

1/4 teaspoon ground nutmeg

Instructions

1. Beat together sugar, brown sugar, oil, eggs, sour cream, and apple cider. Stir in almonds.

2. In another bowl, sift together flour, baking powder, and spices.

3. Add flour mixture to batter a little at a time until it is combined and has formed a soft dough.

4. On floured surface, shape dough into a roll 14–16 inches long. Put roll on a well-greased baking sheet, and flatten to about 3/4 of an inch.

5. Bake 25 minutes in a 375-degree oven.

6. Cool 10 minutes. Then cut into slices about 3/4 of an inch wide. Bake 10 minutes more.

Makes approximately 24 biscotti.

$\mathcal{L}$iz, you've got to help me."

Mary Alice and I have been friends for a long time. And I've heard lots of different emotions in her voice. Surprise. Excitement. Delight. Embarrassment. Anxiety. Even panic. But I've never heard this kind of desperation.

"M.A., what's wrong? Are you okay?" I begin to pace back and forth in my kitchen.

"Yes, of course. I mean, no—"

"Slow down. Take a deep breath and tell me what's going on." I sound just like Jess. I better be careful before I start crowing like Marina.

"I've done something really foolish. Something I knew I'd regret as soon as I did it. But I couldn't help myself. You're the only one I could call."

Me? The only one she could call? This doesn't happen to me very often—unless it's my kids when they've forgotten their lunch or when John needs me to pick up his dry cleaning before the store closes.

But this is different. Lizzie to the rescue? I could get used to this. "You know I'm always here for you, M.A. How can I help?"

"I've had second thoughts about throwing away those letters from my father. I don't know what I was thinking. It was just such a hard day."

I can hear Mary Alice's quiet sobs on the other end of the phone line. It breaks my heart. "It had to be emotionally draining."

"Liz, I *need* to get those letters back. Do you think they might still be in the dumpster?"

"There's only one way to find out. Can you be ready in twenty minutes?"

Liz in charge. It has a nice ring to it.

●

$\mathcal{I}$n the midst of my enthusiasm over this new can-do attitude, I forget all about John and his "flu/cold." I needn't have worried. His channel surfing has netted a rerun of *Monster House*, and he is happily watching the crew transform a suburban tract home into an Outback Oasis. Right now the crew is mounting a huge crocodile head over the deck as an awning.

"Sweetheart, I need to run out with Mary Alice for about an hour. Will you be okay?"

"Is there any more soup left?"

"A whole pot."

John smiles. "Then I'll be fine."

●

*K*nowing where we were headed this time, Mary Alice and I zipped right past the manager's office at Storage Unlimited and pulled up next to the dumpster near her storage unit. Unfortunately, I forgot about the pesky speed bump in the parking lot—probably placed to discourage just this sort of "zippy" driving—and spilled coffee down the front of my sweatshirt. But that's a small price to pay for the cups of Cinnamon Dream Mocha and an Apple Almond Biscotti we picked up at a coffee shop on the way. After all, dumpster-diving is hard work.

I dabbed at my sweatshirt with a napkin and started to open the car door. "We might as well get this over with."

Mary Alice put her hand on my arm. "How about if we pray first?"

Why didn't I think of that? Some leader I'm turning out to be. "Good idea. You start and I'll finish."

We clasp hands and bow our heads.

"Lord, you know I've prayed many times for answers about my father. For closure. For acceptance. And when you answered me, I ignored it. Going so far as to toss it away." Mary Alice wipes away a tear. "Lord, although I don't deserve it, please forgive me. And help me find my father's letters."

Being in charge isn't what it's cracked up to be. How am I supposed to pray with a huge lump in my throat? As tears slip down my face and fall on our clasped hands, I long for Jess or Lucy to take over. Even Kelly or Marina.

"Lord, I agree with everything Mary Alice said," I manage to croak. "In Jesus's name, amen."

As Mary Alice and I get out of my minivan, I realize that Liz and leader may start with the same letter—but they are not on the same page.

That's an issue to consider another day. Our immediate problem is the huge blue dumpster looming before us.

I stretch up on tiptoes and peer over the edge of the monstrosity. "Well, it doesn't look like it's been emptied yet. But I have no idea how we're going to find anything without climbing in."

"I wish I would have thought to bring a stepladder." Mary Alice hands me a pair of rubber gloves from her bag and then puts on another pair herself. "Let's put these on before we touch anything."

I snap on one of the thick gloves. "You think of everything, don't you?"

"I certainly didn't think about how we were going to get into the dumpster. I assumed the letters would be on top. Are you sure you don't see them? They were tied with a pink ribbon."

Mary Alice joins me on tiptoe at the side of the dumpster, her eyes barely reaching above the edge. With her sleek ponytail, chartreuse cardigan, and navy capris, she doesn't fit the typical picture of a dumpster diva. Even with the bright blue plastic gloves on her hands. I, on the other hand, dressed in an old gray sweatshirt (now enhanced with coffee stains) and my "fat jeans," probably fit the profile perfectly.

After several minutes of futilely scanning the contents, I decide to move back into leadership mode. "If you give me a boost, I could climb in."

"Oh no, Liz. That's too dangerous. And who knows what's in that filthy dumpster? If anything, I should be the one to get in."

I glance over my shoulder at my friend. Mary Alice has the prune-face of a toddler who's taken his first bite of peas.

I point to her shoes. "Not in those Cole Haan mules, you're not."

Mary Alice looks down at her feet. "I guess I didn't dress very appropriately, did I?"

"No, but I did. So give me a boost and I'll fish out those letters."

It doesn't take long for me to understand why they call it dumpster-diving. The only way I can make it into the container is to tumble in. Once inside, I know I'll pay for my exploits with bruises and sore muscles.

At least I have the chicken soup ready.

Two-thirds of the long container is covered with a metal lid, blocking out much of the natural light and keeping in the fetid odor. I recognize a couple of the trash bags we tossed into the dumpster on Saturday. But there's no sign of the packet of letters.

Mary Alice's voice outside the dumpster sounds flat and muffled. "Liz, are you all right?"

I bend down and peer into the darkness in an effort to spot the pale pink ribbon Mary Alice's dad had tied around his letters to Maya. "I'm okay, but it's hard to see in here."

"I have a flashlight in my purse. I'll get it from the car."

Of course Mary Alice would have a flashlight in her purse. Along with a sewing kit, nail file, address book—and probably a nonperishable dinner for eight. The U.S. Department of Homeland Security has nothing on this woman.

I continue to poke around in the dumpster, gingerly lifting pieces of cardboard. Then I spot the hibachi! It's just out of my reach under some old newspapers. Maybe if I take a step—

Yikes! The sharp clang of metal banging on the side of the dumpster causes me to cover my ears. "Hey! Watch it, M.A.! It's like an echo chamber in here." Annoyed, I stand up and look over the edge.

The culprit is not Mary Alice at all. It's one of Omaha's Finest in his crisp blue uniform.

"Ma'am, I'm going to have to ask you to step out of the dumpster. And please keep your hands where I can see them."

●

*M*ary Alice and I are sitting in the backseat of a black-and-white police cruiser. A piece of thick Plexiglas separates us from the officer in the front seat. There are no handles on the doors. And the odor . . . let's just say it's unpleasant.

Mary Alice's face is pale, her voice trembling. "Liz, I'm so sorry about all this. I had no idea dumpster-diving was illegal."

"You wouldn't think it would be. Especially when you're diving for your own stuff."

I'm having trouble believing this is actually happening, especially after Mary Alice explained that she was a customer and rented one of the storage units. But the manager refused to withdraw the complaint, citing problems with "riffraff who think just because something is in the trash it's free."

Interesting concept.

So here we are, like two rabbits in a trap while Officer Friendly calls in our driver's license numbers to make sure we aren't on the FBI's Most Wanted List. Unless . . .

I knock on the Plexiglas. "Excuse me? Officer?"

The young cop slides open a little window in the partition so he can hear us. "Yes, ma'am?"

It's time to play the Marina card. "You know, Officer, I just thought of someone who might be able to clear this whole thing up. In fact, she was with us on Saturday and is aware of the entire situation. Marina Favazza. *Lieutenant* Marina Favazza."

The officer doesn't bother to turn around. Instead he eyes me warily in the rearview mirror. "You know the Lieut?"

This might work. "She's a dear friend. And as I said, Lieutenant Favazza was with us on Saturday assisting our friend here as she sorted through the effects of her deceased father."

"I'll call in." The officer slides the door in the window shut.

Mary Alice jumps at the sound. "Oh Liz, do you think Marina will be upset that we dragged her into this? I mean, if what we were doing was illegal—"

I roll my eyes. "For goodness' sake! We weren't trying to steal anything. All we were doing was trying to get back *your stuff.*"

"Well, if you think she won't be mad—"

The little door in the Plexiglas shoots open again before Mary Alice can finish her sentence. "Ladies, do you have someone who could come pick up your car? Otherwise, I'll need to have it towed."

Towed? What's going on here?

A bead of sweat creeps down the side of my face. "I'm sorry, Officer, I don't understand. Did you reach Lieutenant Favazza?"

"Yep, I talked to her. She said to bring both of you in."

chAPTER TWENTY

HOMEMADE TWINKIES

1 yellow cake mix (prepared and baked according to directions
   on the box)

5 tablespoons flour

1 cup milk

1/2 cup vegetable shortening

1/2 cup butter (room temperature)

1/2 teaspoon salt

1 teaspoon vanilla

1 cup white sugar

Instructions

1. Prepare cake mix according to directions in a 9x13-inch pan.
   Cool thoroughly.

2. Using a long knife, cut cake in half lengthwise. For bottom
   layer, place 1 half on a cookie sheet or jelly-roll pan lined
   with wax paper.

3. Whisk flour into milk in a saucepan. Heat until thickened,
   stirring constantly. Cool.

4. Beat together remaining ingredients (shortening, butter,
   salt, vanilla, and sugar) until fluffy. Slowly beat in cooled
   flour/milk mixture.

5. Spread filling on the bottom layer. Top with remaining layer.
   Refrigerate.

6. To serve, cut into bars.

FRIED TWINKIES

6 Twinkies

4 cups vegetable oil

1 cup flour

1 teaspoon baking powder

1/2 teaspoon salt

1 cup milk

2 tablespoons vinegar

1 tablespoon oil

6 Popsicle sticks

Flour for dusting

Instructions:

1. Freeze Twinkies until frozen solid (several hours or overnight).
2. Heat vegetable oil in deep fryer or deep frying pan to 375 degrees.
3. In small bowl, mix flour, baking powder, and salt. Add milk, vinegar, and oil. Mix until smooth. Chill.
4. To fry Twinkies: Push a Popsicle stick lengthwise into each Twinkie. Leave about 2 inches for a handle.
5. Dust Twinkie with flour and dip in batter. Be sure to rotate so batter coats entire Twinkie.
6. Fry in hot oil, using a spoon or spatula to hold cake down so it doesn't float and browns evenly.
7. When golden brown, remove Twinkie from oil and let drain on a paper towel. Allow to cool for 5 minutes before serving.
8. This is also good served with a chocolate, lemon, or raspberry sauce.

The good news is that Mary Alice and I aren't in handcuffs as we are ushered into the downtown office of the Omaha Police Department. The bad news is that my pastor is visiting detainees in the adjacent holding cells.

"Liz? Mrs. Harris? Is that you?" The poor man looks ready to stroke out any minute.

I flash a weak smile as we pass in the narrow hallway. "Pastor Tom. Hello."

"Keep moving, Mrs. Harris." I feel our arresting officer's hand on my elbow.

"It's not what you think," I call back to the clergyman with mortification written all over his face. "Really, Pastor Tom, it's not."

I am never going to agree to be the one in charge again. I don't care what the situation, leadership is not my gift. Just look at us. Poor Mary Alice is almost catatonic. She hasn't said a word since finding out we were being brought to the station. And my pastor is probably already on his cell phone alerting the prayer team about my "unfortunate situation."

Maybe I am in *The Twilight Zone*. At this point, even Rod Serling would be a welcome sight.

●

So how are the two jailbirds doing?" Marina, dressed in her blue uniform, holds the door to her office open for us. "I'll take it from here, Joe," she says to the officer who brought us in.

Mary Alice stares at Marina with wide eyes. "Are you the one who is going to book us?"

Marina's "cop face" shatters into raucous laughter. "Gotcha!"

Gotcha? Gotcha! Is this a joke?

Mary Alice's throat is trembling so much it appears she's swallowed a frog. "What—"

"No, you didn't, Marina! No, you didn't!" I have an intense urge to strangle my practical-joking friend.

"You've been punk'd, baby!" she sputters.

I am not amused.

Still apparently unable to control her laughter, Marina motions for us to sit in the two chairs in front of her black metal desk. She sinks into the high-backed office chair behind it.

Mary Alice shoots me a thin smile. "It is kind of funny when you step back and look at it."

"Don't encourage her, Mary Alice." I turn away and look at the bookcases that line one wall of the office. Interspersed between drooping plants and family photos are an array of binders and several textbooks with imposing names. *Criminal Law for the Criminal Justice Professional. Statistical Methods for Criminology. Criminal Investigation.* Maybe when you deal with subjects this heavy each day, a little levity keeps life in perspective. And she did get us. Very good.

Marina finally composes herself. "Can I get you a cup of coffee after your ordeal? It pretty much stinks by this time of day but—"

I sigh. "One question. Why?"

Marina rests her elbows on her desk. "After Joey called, I figured out what you were after in the dumpster. I thought it'd be easier to have you come here."

Mary Alice stiffens. "I don't understand."

Me neither.

Marina gets up and opens the top drawer of the file cabinet behind her desk. After rummaging around in the back, she finds what she's looking for.

The letters. Still tied with the faded pink ribbon.

●

I knew you'd want these back eventually." Marina rocks back in her chair.

Misty-eyed, Mary Alice is cradling the packet of envelopes in her lap, fingering the frayed satin ribbon. "But how? You left before we did."

Marina snorts. "That was just a diversion. I went back and snagged the letters from the dumpster."

That's why I found the hibachi—but no letters.

"So am I forgiven for having you hauled in?" Marina pushes back her chair and props her feet on the desk.

I concede a small smile. "We might forgive you, but John—who is sick by the way—is the one who had to miss *Monster House* to pick up my car. He's probably on his way to get us. That is, if we can make bail."

Marina laughs. "Quick, call him. My shift ends at three. I'll take you home. Unless you're up for a little dinner first?"

Mary Alice speaks up. "I should pass. The kids will be home in an hour and—"

"Then give me the letters." Marina holds out her hand across the desk.

"What?" Mary Alice appears to be as confused as I am.

"You heard me. Hand 'em over."

I decide to speak up. "You already got us once today, Rina. Lay off."

Marina plops her feet back on the floor. "I'm not kidding. There's some heavy stuff in there. M.A. will need one of us around when she reads them."

Did she just say what I think she did?

"Marina! You didn't read Mary Alice's letters, did you?"

"Of course I read 'em."

Mary Alice's jaw drops. My face must also reflect the mixture of shock and outrage that's brewing inside since Marina scrambles to explain her reasoning.

"My dad used to call hippies 'pot-smoking, acid-dropping, free-sex commie traitors.' I had to be sure your dad wasn't one of those types before I turned over the letters." Marina slaps her forehead. "I forgot. Jeff told me not to mention the stuff about pot-smoking, acid-dropping, free-sex—"

I pop up from my seat. "You told Jeff!"

Marina shrugs. "I had to. He's the sensitive one."

Mary Alice looks stunned—face pale, arms crossed tightly across her chest.

I'm fuming, not sure what to say, as I drop back into my chair.

Marina turns to Mary Alice. "You're not mad, are you, M.A.? I wanted to be sure there wasn't anything in the letters that might push you over the edge. I didn't want you to go all Stepford on us and start making those Homemade Twinkies again."

A smile flickers in Mary Alice's eyes. "Marina, you are definitely an original. I *am* a bit put out. But I know your intentions were good."

"So you still love me?" Marina flutters her thick, black eyelashes.

"On one condition. That you teach me how to make those horrendous Fried Twinkies my kids had at your house over the holidays. They can't quit talking about them."

"I'll give you the recipe over dinner?"

"How can I refuse when junk food is at stake? I'll call Craig and see if he can take the kids out for pizza tonight. I'd like to see what you found so fascinating in my letters."

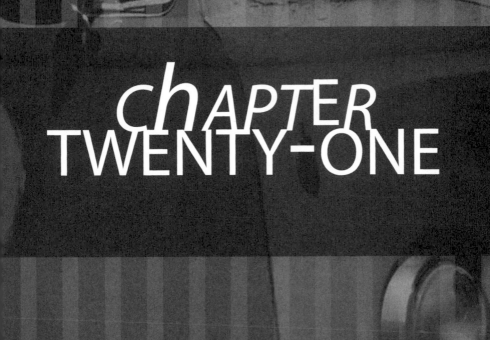

chAPTER
TWENTY-ONE

JORGE'S CHICKEN FAJITAS

1 1/2 pounds boneless skinless chicken strips

2 large onions, sliced

3 tablespoons oil

3 tablespoons lime juice

1 green bell pepper, sliced

1 red bell pepper, sliced

3/4 cup salsa

2 cloves garlic, minced

8 tortillas

Toppings

Sour cream

Guacamole (recipe below)

Pica de gallo (recipe below)

Instructions

1. Combine all ingredients except tortillas and toppings in plastic bag. Marinate 2–24 hours.

2. Cook in a skillet over medium heat.

3. Serve with warmed tortillas and toppings.

SPICY GUACAMOLE

Combine:

1 large ripe avocado, peeled and mashed

2 tablespoons mayonnaise

1 tomato, diced

1/4 cup lemon juice

1/4 cup finely diced red onion

Salt and pepper to taste

PICA DE GALLO

Combine:

2 red onions, diced

4 ripe tomatoes, diced

1/3 cup chopped cilantro

3 jalapenos, diced

1/4 cup fresh orange juice

1/4 cup fresh lime juice

Salt and pepper to taste

Serves 4–6.

*I*n typical FAC fashion, the words comfort and food go together. Mary Alice needs comfort and, in this case, the food to provide it is Tex-Mex. Instead of eating at the restaurant, we decide on carry-out and head to Marina's house.

"So where are the girls?" I ask, referring to Marina's twelve-year-old twins, Amy and Kim.

"Debate tournament. No parents allowed."

I set the bag of food on Marina's colorful tile counter and remove the containers of Chicken Fajitas, Spicy Guacamole, and Pica de Gallo. "Do the two of them ever compete against each other?"

"Just in practice. And boy, are they competitive."

"Wonder where they get that from?" I ask.

Marina ignores my comment and yanks stiff paper plates and plastic cups from her dark wood cabinets. "I'm using the good stuff for you ladies."

Mary Alice laughs. She has relaxed considerably since our ordeal at the police station. And the laid-back atmosphere of Marina's house with her big cushy sectional and the huge leather ottoman that invites putting your feet up is a perfect remedy for a stressful day.

We fill paper plates and head to the family room.

"Good choice, Lizzie," says Mary Alice. "I haven't had Jorge's Chicken Fajitas for ages."

"He makes the best in town." As Marina takes a big bite, guacamole oozes out one end of the tortilla.

I wipe my mouth with a napkin. "Yeah, but how much competition do you really have for Tex-Mex in Nebraska?"

"Hispanics are the fastest growing population in the state." Mary Alice takes a sip of her diet pop.

"What? Next to prairie dogs?" teases Marina.

Mary Alice and I both give Marina a disapproving look. Although neither of us is a native Nebraskan, we've come to love the state. It's a wonderful place to raise a family. Great schools. Reasonable cost of living. And Omaha offers all the amenities of a big city without the headaches of traffic and high crime. We won't have Marina dissing Nebraska. No matter how much Ted Drewes frozen custard she brings us from her trips back to her hometown of St. Louis.

I am trying to think of a clever retort when the doorbell rings. "Are you expecting anyone?" I ask.

Before she can answer, we hear the front door open.

Marina stands up. "Who's there?" she barks.

"Goodness, Marina. It's just me." Kelly appears around the corner. "I thought we had a 'no need to knock' policy in FAC."

Marina plops back on the sofa and puts her feet up. "It's Monday, in case you haven't noticed."

"Exactly. So why are you guys getting together without inviting me?" Kelly can sniff out a situation like a bloodhound. It's uncanny.

"How did you know we were here?" I ask.

"I called your house, and John filled me in on the whole sordid tale. How *could* you, Marina? And Liz—*dumpster-diving?*"

I might as well face up to the fact that this will haunt me for years. Leapin' Lizzie the Dumpster-Diver.

●

So, shall we read the first letter?" Kelly has usurped my role as leader. I'm thrilled.

"Now that I have my dad's letters, I'm scared to find out what he wrote." Mary Alice chews her bottom lip. "Maybe I don't really want to know . . ."

Kelly moves to the edge of the sofa. "Of course you want to know. Otherwise you wouldn't have let Liz risk her life in that dumpster."

Whoa! Kelly's playing the guilt card. And few things motivate Mary Alice more than guilt.

Kelly doesn't let up. "So, do you want to read them, or shall I?"

Mary Alice pauses before answering. "I'd rather Lizzie read them."

Kelly raises an eyebrow and sits back on the sofa. Marina gives me a silent thumbs-up.

How did I end up as leader of the pack again? Is God trying to push me out of my comfort zone? I carefully untie the ribbon and slip out a yellowed envelope from the top of the pile. I ease out the two brittle sheets from the envelope and begin reading.

August 30, 1968

Dear Maya,

I can't believe I'm not with you—my beautiful little girl—on your first birthday. I hope one day you will be able to forgive me. Right now the only thing I can think to do is to write you this letter. A letter I can't mail . . .

●

"Denny sat in the stark jail cell not knowing what to do. He couldn't bring himself to call Ali and tell her where he was—and why he was there. Tensions were already strained with his parents since he'd dropped out of college. This would only make things worse. And there was no phone at Avalon. Even if he got in touch with someone at the commune, no one had the two hundred bucks to bail him out of jail.

This was not supposed to happen.

The tired-looking public defender a federal judge had appointed to represent Denny said he was charged with crossing state lines with the intent to incite a riot.

"That's bogus!" Denny had told him. "I came to Chicago to let the fat cats in Washington know that the people demand an end to this war. It was the Chicago cops who began busting heads and started the riot. I barely got out of there alive."

"Then why is your signature on a receipt from Central Scientific for the purchase of"—the lawyer rifled through his stack of papers—"butyric acid? The prosecutor says that's a chemical used to make stink bombs. The same kind that were set off on Michigan Avenue."

Now, as Denny contemplated the lawyer's words, the walls seemed to close in around him. He was shaken from his thoughts by the banging of a nightstick on the bars of his cell.

"Hey O'Brien, let's go," the rotund prison guard ordered. "You made bail."

"Me?" Denny scrambled from the cot he was sitting on. "Are you sure?"

"I don't see any other long-haired freaks around here named Dennis O'Brien. Do you?" The guard used the keys hanging from his belt to unlock the cell door.

Denny was sure there had to be a mistake. He hadn't even used his one phone call. "It's just that—"

The guard scowled. "I don't have time for this, O'Brien. Do you wanna go home—or stay in here with your girlfriends?"

●

Kevin's ginger-colored Afro and huge smile was hard to miss as Denny pushed through the swinging gate into the lobby of Cook County Jail.

"Hey man, how's it hangin'?" The tall man stretched out his hand to shake Denny's.

"Not too bad. When'd you get out?"

"Earlier this morning. This place makes San Quentin look like a resort."

"It's been a real bummer." Denny shoved his wallet in his back pocket and tossed the bag that had held it into a nearby trash can. "You have any idea who posted my bail?"

Kevin glanced around the busy lobby. "Yeah, but let's split. Then we can talk."

"I'm down with that. I can't get out of this hole too soon."

The two men walked through the revolving doors of the jail that had held some of the country's most notorious criminals through the years, from mobster Al Capone to serial killer John Wayne Gacy. The stifling August heat assaulted them, making Denny long for a shower and a good night's sleep.

"You got any wheels, man?" asked Kevin.

"Yeah, Camille—my van—is parked not too far from Old Town."

"Let's go get her. A meeting is going down out in the country—near Downers Grove. You'll understand everything once we get there."

●

Denny counted twenty-three people gathered in the living room of the old farmhouse in Downers Grove including Rob, Kristin, and squirrelly Dwayne. The house wasn't decorated in typical hippie-style with floor pillows, Indian blankets, and beads. Instead the stark walls and lack of furniture gave it the air of being abandoned. The only hint that the house might be inhabited by more than mice was the rusty folding table and chairs in the kitchen and a few stained mattresses with sleeping bags on the floor.

A man with shoulder-length hair, tied back in a ponytail with a leather thong, greeted Kevin and Denny with the unity handshake. "Hey man, glad you're here. Make yourselves comfortable. We're just getting started."

"Who was that?" Denny whispered as he and Kevin sat, knees to their chests, on the crowded floor of the living room.

"I saw him at a couple of SDS meetings, but I don't remember his name."

Denny studied the others crammed into the small room. All were young, white—and with the exception of Dwayne—obviously well-mannered. He felt the electricity of anticipation in the air.

A compact man who appeared to be in his midtwenties stood to address the group. His tight, dark curls were kept out of his face by a headband with Free the People printed on it.

"Are you glad to be free from the fist of the corrupt Chicago Police Department?" the man asked, pumping his fist in the air.

A chorus of "Right on!" and "Power to the people!" came from the crowd.

The speaker continued. "Some of you may be wondering why you are here . . . instead of in jail. You're wondering who put up your bail. I want you to know that your efforts on behalf of The Movement have not gone unnoticed."

Denny's confusion grew as another round of "Right on!" bounced around the room. *Could this mean that this guy—or this group—posted bail for me? They don't even know me. What's the catch?*

"After what went down this week both inside and outside the Convention," the speaker continued, "it's more apparent than ever that the democratic political process in this country has fallen apart. And it's been replaced by a police state that's willing to do whatever it takes to keep power from the people."

A cry of "Kill the fascist pigs!" blasted from the back of the room. Denny turned and wasn't surprised to see the shout had come from Dwayne. He seemed almost giddy with excitement. Spittle flecked the corners of his mouth, and there was a wildness in his eyes.

"I hate to admit that it's come down to that," said the speaker, acknowledging Dwayne with the closed fist symbolizing Black Power, "but it's obvious that nonviolent methods are not working to bring about crucial change in our society. Today we are faced with the same choice of patriots that came before us. To fight for what we believe in—or be wiped out."

"Fight! Fight! Fight!" The chant of the crowd filled the small room, reminding Denny of the frenzy just before violence exploded on Michigan Avenue.

The speaker put his arms up to quiet the group. "You need to know that we didn't come to this conclusion easily. We tried to follow the example of Dr. King and the principles of Gandhi by planning nonviolent protests. But

Mayor Daley violated our constitutional right to protest by refusing to grant permits. This, coupled with the actions on the part of the Chicago Police when demonstrators tried to exercise their civil rights, leaves us no choice but to take up arms."

"So the question I have for you today, people, is this—will you be a patriot or a patsy?"

●

By the next morning, the group was dividing into squads of four or five people who had agreed to go underground and work for The Movement. This meant no contact with family or friends not in the organization. It also meant skipping their respective court dates, which automatically made them federal fugitives.

Denny was sitting alone on a stack of old tires in back of the farmhouse when the speaker from yesterday came out the back door and sat next to him.

"I hear you still haven't made up your mind. It's good that you're not taking the call lightly."

Denny gazed out at the dusty, weed-choked yard. "Man, I'm down with The Cause, but I've got a wife and a kid. I don't see how I can go underground."

"That was my concern when Rob approached me about bringing you into the organization. But he convinced me that your knowledge of chemistry was a crucial asset." His intense dark eyes locked with Denny's. "The People need someone with your skills, Denny."

"I know, but I can't leave my wife and little girl—"

"I don't think you realize the situation, Denny. You're charged with a federal crime. A felony. So regardless of the choice you make, you're going to leave your family. You just need to decide if you want to spend it working for The Movement . . . or rotting in Cook County Jail."

●

Denny felt heavy as he waited to begin the long trip from Chicago to Northern California with Kevin. His heaviness didn't come from a physical burden—but the burden of his decision. Would Ali and Maya understand that he had no choice? Would they ever forgive him?

The speaker leaned against Camille and relayed last-minute instructions. "You need to find a place to crash that's within an hour's drive of San Francisco. Make sure it's quiet—but someplace where you'll blend in."

Kevin laughed. "That shouldn't be too hard in California."

The man handed Denny a manila envelope. "Here's some bread to help you get settled. Rob, Kristin, and Dwayne will meet you at the corner of Haight and Ashbury at noon on October 1. They'll have contact information and further instructions for your squad."

As he and Kevin climbed into Camille, Denny realized the speaker had never told him his name. Stranger still, he had never thought to ask.

●

After Chicago I changed from being a pacifist to the realization we have to defend ourselves. Although I desperately wish the opposite was true, I know deep in my soul that a nonviolent revolution is impossible. And I can't stand by and let the country slip into this cesspool of fascism.

I am committed to do whatever it takes to make a better world for you and your mom. I'm still not sure what that will mean—and I don't expect you to understand—but please know that I love you. Happy birthday, sweet baby.

Love always,

Daddy

As I hand the letter to Mary Alice, silence blankets the room like a cloud.

After what seems like several minutes, Mary Alice speaks. "Now I know. I still don't understand. But at least I know."

I sit forward on Marina's sectional. "You want me to read the next letter? Maybe there's some more explanation."

"Not right now. I think I need to talk to my mom. Maybe she can fill in the blanks."

Kelly, Marina, and I are uncharacteristically quiet as the unspoken question hangs in the air.

Mary Alice looks up, a small smile on her face. "And yes, you can come to Rock Port with me."

chapter
TWENTY-TWO

LAVENDER LEMONADE

1 cup sugar

4 cups water

8–10 stems fresh lavender

2 cups lemon juice (fresh is best)*

* Hint: To get the most juice out of a lemon, you need to warm it up. To do this, you can either roll the lemon on a hard surface a few times, pressing down with the palm of your hand, or put it in the microwave for 25 seconds.

Instructions

1. Boil sugar with half the water until sugar is completely dissolved. Remove from heat.
2. Steep the lavender stems in sugar water at least 30 minutes.
3. Add rest of water and lemon juice. Strain to remove lavender.
4. Serve over ice and garnish with lavender blossoms.

Serves 6–8.

GRAM'S FRUIT COCKTAIL CAKE

1 cup all-purpose flour

1 cup sugar

1 teaspoon baking powder

1/4 teaspoon salt

1 large egg, beaten until light

2 cups fruit cocktail with juice

1 teaspoon vanilla extract

1 cup firmly packed brown sugar

1/4 cup (1/2 stick) butter

1/2 cup chopped walnuts or pecans

Whipped cream (optional)

Instructions

1. Sift flour, sugar, baking powder, and salt into a large bowl.
2. Mix in egg, fruit cocktail, and vanilla.
3. Pour into a 9x13-inch greased pan.
4. Combine brown sugar, butter, and nuts. Sprinkle over top of batter.
5. Bake in a 350-degree oven about 45 minutes or until a toothpick inserted in center comes out clean.
6. Serve with whipped cream, if desired.

I love FAC road trips. I especially like them when Marina drives. She confidently maneuvers both interstates and country roads in her big blue boat of a car. And we never get lost. This may be because, as a police officer, she's logged countless hours behind the wheel. Or maybe she doesn't fear state troopers with their thick books of traffic citations waiting to be filled out. Regardless, it's always relaxing when we leave the driving to Marina.

We were able to take Marina's convertible because only four of us could make the trip to visit Mary Alice's mother. Lucy is on call for her women's shelter at Locust Hill, so she needs to spend the night in Tredway. And Jess is busy packing for a romantic weekend with Michael at a Bed and Breakfast in Jamesport, Missouri. So it's just four of us—Mary Alice, Kelly, Marina, and me—zipping south along I-29 and looking for the Rock Port exit.

I'm not sure what I'm expecting to find in Mary Alice's hometown. Perhaps one of those sleepy little farming communities that are so common in rural areas. The ones with a grain elevator and combination gas station, diner, and minimart. All small towns have character—it's just that in some small communities it's harder to find it.

In Rock Port, character is evident wherever you look. From the Atchison County Courthouse built in 1882 to historic Main Street with its quaint row of antique and specialty shops. Even Mary Alice's childhood home, which sits on the corner of a quiet residential street, resembles something out of a Thomas Kinkade painting.

"Mary Alice, it's beautiful!" My eyes can't drink in enough of the riot of greenery and color that surrounds the white clapboard bungalow with cheery, blue shutters. "Does your mom take care of that garden all by herself?"

Mary Alice laughs. "Now that I'm gone, that's her baby. She pampers the garden like a long-lost child."

Huge bearded iris bloom around the perimeter of a screened porch in the backyard. Bright yellow daffodils and pretty blue hyacinths border the walk. And pots overflowing with colorful pansies decorate the front stoop. The house looks exactly the way I would describe a rose-covered cottage. But without the roses since it's only April.

Marina glances into the backseat at Mary Alice. "So how do we get to your mom's shop? Or is she at home by now?"

"She doesn't lock up until six. Mother runs a special on Friday afternoons to encourage men to pick up flowers for their sweethearts."

I sigh. "Friday flowers. That's so romantic."

"Yeah, yeah," Marina grouses. "But that's not getting us any closer to our destination, is it?"

"Sorry, Marina," says Mary Alice. "Turn left here. It's only three blocks to my mother's shop."

"That's convenient," comments Kelly from the front seat.

"This way Mother can walk to work since she hates to drive. I used to think it was because she's such an environmental zealot. But I've come to the conclusion that she doesn't want to bother with a car. She lives a simple life. And if it's too far to walk—she hops on her bike."

Her bike? I get a flashback of my fateful spinning class and wonder if Mary Alice's mom will end up being one of Marina's buddies from the BRAN.

We find Ali's Garden along Main Street between Cass and Opp. An older woman that Mary Alice points out as her mother is watering the display of potted plants lined up outside the front door.

As pleasantly surprised as I am with the charm of Rock Port, I am even more surprised when I meet Ali O'Brien. Ever since hearing that

Mary Alice's mom was a flower child, I had formed a picture of a flamboyant woman with long silver hair. Maybe wearing a long, fringed vest. Or at least a poncho. I was certain her feet would be clad in a pair of Birkenstocks glowing with the patina of age.

The woman Mary Alice introduces looks like she stepped out of a Gap advertisement in her khakis and loose white blouse with the sleeves rolled up. And I'd bet my chocolate stash that her shoes have the same style number as my Naturalizer slip-ons.

Ali, as she insists we call her, is petite like Mary Alice—almost birdlike. She has short, wispy blond hair, streaked with silver. Her intelligent green eyes are framed by rimless, oval glasses.

Ali takes Kelly's hand in both her own after Mary Alice makes introductions. "Maya has told me so much about you. She says you're such a gifted therapist. And very inspirational."

Kelly looks a little embarrassed. "That was sweet of her to say. Especially since I can be a little pushy at times."

"Well, we all need a little shove now and then, don't we?" Ali smiles and turns to Marina. "My dear, I'd recognize you anywhere!"

Maybe they really are biking buddies.

Marina raises her eyebrows. "Have we met?"

"Not formally, but I recognize you from my granddaughter's team picture. Sally loves you as her soccer coach. In fact, I hope to get up to Omaha for a game one of these days."

Maybe she and Marina can ride their bikes.

"And this must be Liz—the writer!" I am taken a little aback as Ali clasps both my hands and stands back to look at me the way my mom used to do when I was dressed up for a school dance.

"I adore your column, my dear. Maya used to clip it for me. Now I have my own subscription to the Omaha paper." She puts her arm around my shoulder as we follow the others into the shop. "I think you should consider syndicating. Especially with your new focus encouraging women to be themselves. Brilliant!"

It's always so interesting to meet a friend's parent and to hear what she's told them about you. I had no idea M.A. sent her mom my columns. I am flattered–and a little disconcerted. It's also more than a little disconcerting to hear Ali refer to Mary Alice as Maya. Now I'm not sure what to call her myself. I don't want to offend someone who appears to be my biggest fan. After all, I had read *Misery* and knew all about the gruesome treatment of a writer by his biggest fan.

I shiver and notice Ali looking at me quizzically. "Is everything all right, dear?"

"Yes, I'm fine. I was just thinking of a book I once read."

In the few minutes we've spoken, you can certainly tell Mary Alice is Ali's daughter. Not only do they resemble each other physically with their small frames and light coloring, they both have a keen intuition. They are also the type of woman who cares enough to remember the details about other people's lives. And to use those details to encourage them. As one who has trouble remembering her cell phone number, I know this is not a gift to be taken lightly.

Neither is Ali's gift for merchandising. The shop is a whimsical array of flowers and gifts to delight even the most dour customer. And the flowers smell heavenly, reminding me of the Herbal Essences shampoo I used as a teenager. From colorful pots to funky note cards, I could spend hours—and way too much money—in this shopper's paradise.

"Now come, girls." Ali shoos us toward a beaded doorway separating the shop from another room. "Let's go into the back room so we can chat. McGovern will come to get me if a customer wanders in."

As if on cue, the cat leaps to the wide front windowsill and curls up to enjoy the late afternoon sun.

As Ali holds the beaded curtain aside to allow us to enter the back room, Mary Alice walks over to the window and strokes the silver-flecked fur of the calico cat. "Have you been keeping an eye on Mother for me, McGovern? You know I'm counting on you to keep her out of trouble."

Ali laughs. "Trust me, Maya, that old cat is going to get me *into* trouble if he doesn't stay out of the Cramers' flowerbeds. I told them not to plant catnip, but does anyone listen to me?"

Ali's back room doesn't look like any back room I've come across. I was expecting stacks of boxes, fixtures—and maybe a cluttered desk. But this room is quite cozy and reminds me of an old-fashioned sun porch. The comfortable-looking loveseat and armchairs are covered with colorful quilts. A vase of red tulips sits on an antique wooden chest that serves as a coffee table.

Ali sets a frosty pitcher on the chest next to glasses and a bowl of ice. "This is a new recipe I came up with. The lemonade is flavored with lavender from my garden. I'll be anxious to hear what you think."

Mary Alice and Kelly sit down on the loveseat to Ali's left. I decide to curl up in one of the armchairs, and Marina settles next to me on a boldly patterned floor pillow.

Marina takes the glass of the Lavender Lemonade Ali offers her. "Herbal lemonade. Huh." She sniffs and takes a sip.

"So what's the verdict, Marina?" Ali asks.

"Not bad. Not bad at all."

"Coming from you, I take that as a high compliment. Maya told me about your delicious cannolis."

"Well, they're actually my mom's recipe. She's the real cook in the family."

Is Marina blushing? I quickly come to my senses and surmise that the two red spots blooming on her cheeks *have* to be a reaction to the lavender.

Ali spoons a dollop of whipped cream on a piece of golden cake she has sitting on a side table. "The recipe for this cake is from my mother, too." She hands the plate to Mary Alice with a fork and napkin. "Do you recognize it, Maya?"

Mary Alice grins at her mother. "It's Gram's Fruit Cocktail Cake. Thank you for making it, Mother."

Ali passes another plate of the gooey, whipped-cream-laden cake to Kelly. "Before she died, my mother made this cake every year for Maya's birthday—much to my chagrin. It's full of preservatives and has nothing even remotely nutritional. But it was her granddaughter's favorite cake, and Mom wasn't about to let a birthday slip by without it."

Mary Alice reaches over and squeezes her mother's shoulder. "The last three years you've baked it for me."

"It's tradition. But don't blame me if all the chemicals in here cause you to wake up one night and discover you glow in the dark."

Kelly stops her fork midway between her plate and mouth and looks at the cake suspiciously. After a moment she puts the fork on the plate and sets it aside.

Ali laughs. "See, Maya? Your friend Kelly's a smart chick."

"No, it's not that," sputters Kelly, obviously unaware that anyone had noticed what she'd done. "It's just—"

Mary Alice holds up her hand to stop Kelly's words. "You couldn't have paid my mother a higher compliment by deciding to pass on the cake. That is, unless you took it outside and stomped it into the dirt."

"Are you forgetting what that cake might do to the groundwater?" Ali winks at her daughter. "Am I going to have to send you some more of my ecofriendly pamphlets, Maya?"

Mary Alice laughs and wipes a pearl of whipped cream from the tip of her nose. "Please don't! I've already had enough teasing about my knowledge of the many uses for vinegar around the house. Now you all know who it came from."

It's so strange to see Mary Alice banter with her mother. She almost seems like a different person. Much more relaxed. Even funny. I wonder if it's because she can be herself. Mothers have an uncanny knack for seeing right through their children's masks. Like most adult children, Mary Alice probably knows there's no use trying to put one on when Mom's around.

"Ladies, now that I've plied you with sweets, I'd like to know what prompted this delightful visit."

I almost choke on my cake. *Didn't Mary Alice tell her mom why we're here?*

Ali continues. "I mean, I always wanted to meet Maya's posse but—"

Now it's Mary Alice's turn to choke. "Posse? Mother, where in the world did you hear that word?"

Ali grins mischievously. "I have grandkids, my dear. I need to stay up on the latest lingo."

Mary Alice shakes her head. "My mother, the gangsta."

"That's right, homegirl." Ali punctuates her words with the splayed fingered gestures popular among urban youth.

I laugh—and slosh lemonade on my linen slacks. *I really should consider buying stock in a company that makes stain removers.*

"Seriously, what's the reason for this unexpected visit? It can't be just to show off my garden—even though it's already a feast for the eyes."

I smile. I see so much of Mary Alice in her mom . . . when M.A.'s not on guard. Curiosity. Creativity. A love for making beautiful spaces. Even the twinkle in her eye. Unfortunately, the twinkle only lasts as long as her daughter's next words.

"I'm here to talk about Daddy."

chapter
TWENTY-THREE

CORN BREAD HEAVEN

2 boxes Jiffy cornbread mix

2 eggs

2/3 cup milk

1 (16 ounce) can cream-style corn

1 (16 ounce) can corn, drained

Instructions

1. Mix all ingredients in a bowl.

2. Place in a well-greased 9x13-inch baking pan.

3. Bake at 375 degrees 30–40 minutes or until toothpick inserted in center comes out relatively clean.

HEARTBURN IN A BOWL

2 pounds ground beef

1 large green pepper, chopped

1 large onion, chopped

1 package chili seasoning mix

3 (16 ounce) cans diced tomatoes (do not drain)

2 (16 ounce) cans diced tomatoes, Mexican style (do not drain)

4 (16 ounce) cans kidney beans, drained

2 (16 ounce) cans black beans, drained

1 tablespoon sugar

1 teaspoon ground pepper

Salt to taste

Red pepper to taste

Instructions

1. Brown ground beef with green pepper and onions. Drain off fat.

2. Stir chili seasoning into meat. Add 1 cup water.

3. Add tomatoes, kidney beans, black beans, sugar, and pepper. Simmer 1–3 hours on low.

4. Add salt and red pepper to taste. Enjoy!

Serves 10–12.

$\mathcal{Y}$ou found these in Camille?" Ali runs her fingers over the masculine handwriting on the envelopes Mary Alice had pulled from her bag. The tears on her lashes seem ready to spill over with the slightest provocation.

A little furrow appears between Mary Alice's eyes. "Who's Camille, Mother?"

Ali's response is interrupted by the tinkling of wind chimes strung on the shop door. "I must have a customer." Ali swipes at her eyes with the back of her hand. "Excuse me. I'll just be a minute."

Before slipping through the beaded curtain, Ali pauses to lightly stroke her daughter's hair. Mary Alice responds by leaning into her mother's touch. This simple exchange reminds me that some things will never change, such as the instinct mothers have to protect their babies. Even when those babies have babies of their own.

Kelly refills Mary Alice's glass with lemonade. "I know this is hard, kiddo, but you'll get through it."

Mary Alice responds with a weak smile.

Right now, I wonder if *I'll* make it through the afternoon . . . much less Mary Alice. I hate sticky situations, and from what I've seen through the years, Mary Alice avoids them at all costs. What's worse, there's not a piece of chocolate in sight.

Marina breaks our uneasy silence. "Have you ever talked to your mom about why your dad left?"

"Not really. I broached the subject once, but Mother said it was better if I heard it from my dad. Obviously I never got that chance. But as I got older, I began to think of him as more of a stranger. I guess I began to—what did you call it, Kelly?"

"To detach."

A tear slips down Mary Alice's cheek. "That's it. I began to detach."

●

*I*n a few minutes Ali finishes with her customer and returns to the back room. Her face is a little paler. McGovern is trailing her as if he instinctively knows his mistress needs comfort. The well-fed feline hops into her lap, circling twice before finding the right spot.

Ali strokes the cat's furry back absentmindedly. "So where were we?"

Mary Alice takes a deep breath. "You were going to tell us about some woman named Camille. Who was she, Mother?"

Ali smiles wistfully. "Camille was the name your father gave to his prized possession. A 1963 Volkswagen minibus."

Mary Alice's jaw drops along with the rest of ours. "Camille was his car? He named a car?"

Ali's eyes sparkle at the memory. "It was the thing to do back then."

"I used to call my bike Sparky," I add, taking another bite of cake.

"Why Sparky?" asks Kelly.

Marina smirks. "This oughta be good."

I ignore Marina's jab. "It had a hot pink metallic paint job so she sparkled."

"I shoulda known." Marina snorts. "A Barbie bike. Bet it had a banana seat and one of those pink baskets with the plastic flowers."

It did. But I'm not about to admit it now.

Kelly puts her glass on the table. "What I'm wondering, Liz, is why you felt the bike was female? Was it because of the color? If so, you might be interested in new research that shows colors really are gender neutral—"

"Just forget it." I take another bite of the preservative-laden cake.

Can't a person make a simple comment without getting the third degree?

Ali shuffles through the stack of letters. "Have you read all of these, Maya?"

"I plan to. Eventually."

Ali looks up at her daughter. "Eventually?"

"I have some questions first. That's why I wanted to talk to you." Mary Alice swallows. "Did my father ever come back to explain why he left us?"

Ali closes her eyes and runs her fingers through her short hair. "Once . . ."

●

May 16, 1969

SAN FRANCISCO—Yesterday is now being referred to as "Bloody Thursday" after Governor Ronald Reagan ordered the California National Guard to disperse a crowd of antiwar protesters gathered at Sproul Plaza by spraying tear gas from helicopters. Governor Reagan is quoted as saying, "If it's a bloodbath they want, then let it be now." At least 128 protesters are reported injured.

●

WHEN A NATION IS FILLED WITH STRIFE, THEN DO PATRIOTS FLOURISH.

LAO-TZU

Denny closed the volume of the *I-Ching* he was reading as he waited in the back of Camille. He had parked for the night on a residential street near the University of Kansas in the small town of Lawrence. Even though he was set up with fake ID and corresponding license plates, he'd been trained to do whatever he could to blend in. And there was no better place for a longhair to blend in than on a college campus.

"So how will you see me, Ali? As a patriot—or a punk?" Denny sat up and rubbed his eyes. "I guess it's time to find out."

After stopping at a gas station to splash a little water on his face and brush his teeth, Denny headed north to Rock Port. As he drove, thoughts of the past year floated through his mind like the flickering pictures in an old newsreel . . .

The long trip from Chicago to California along back roads. Panicking every time he and Kevin came under the steady gaze of a local cop or sheriff's deputy. Were they suspicious because they were hippies? Or because they knew? Sleeping fitfully while Kevin drove. Always wondering if the next mile they traveled would be to jail.

Arriving in San Francisco in the middle of September. Just two weeks to find a place to live before the scheduled meeting with Rob, Kristin, and Dwayne. Sleeping wherever they fell.

Setting up house in a dump on the water near Muir Landing. Blending in. But not getting too friendly with the other freaks in the area. Always ready to split at the first sign of trouble.

Missing Ali and Maya. His beautiful girls. Would they ever understand why he couldn't be with them? Did he even understand what he was doing? And why he was doing it?

October 1. Noon. Standing on the corner of Haight and Ashbury. Feeling the sweat bloom on his back even though the air was cool. Where was Rob?

1:30. Sitting on the curb as the madness swirled around him. Trying to be cool. Where were they? Closing his eyes for just a minute . . . Jolted awake by fetid breath close to his face. "Hey man, gotta light?" Dwayne.

Following Dwayne through a maze of people and places to meet up with Rob and Kristin. "Just had to be sure you weren't totin' any pigs, man." Rob with a maniacal gleam in his eyes. Kristin stony-faced. Denny wanting to bag the whole scene. But where would he go?

He was no longer Denny O'Brien. He was Roger Burke. From Evanston, Indiana. Date of birth January 6, 1941. That made him almost 30. Never trust anyone over 30. Especially a mad scientist.

Missing Ali. And Maya. Longing for his old life. Longing for any life. Right now, he didn't exist.

Doing what he was told. Mixing up explosives. Experimenting with packages. Jars. Boxes. Pipes. A good soldier. Not thinking about what the others were doing with his handiwork. This was war. And war was messy. Bloody. He couldn't think about it. Just do your job. Be a good soldier.

Missing Ali. Always missing Ali.

Standing alone in a grove of redwoods in Muir Woods. The ancient trees towering like a cathedral in medieval times. The cool, muffled shadows condemning him like haughty clergymen. "It's too late for you, my boy. Much too late."

Longing for Ali. Missing Maya. Was it too late? Or was there a chance to redeem himself?

Denny turned on Highway 111 for the last leg of his trip. The familiar Midwestern landscape warmed his heart. Would the sight of his face do the same for Ali when she saw him after all these months?

●

"Aren't you going to say something? Ali?"

Denny stood on the stoop of what used to be old lady Anderson's house. It was a white bungalow with a trellis of climbing pink roses on one side. He was separated from his wife by a screen door.

Was Ali going to let him in? Did she even recognize him?

Denny had lost quite a bit of weight the past year due to a combination of nerves and rotten food. And the dark circles under his eyes were now a permanent feature. Maybe he didn't look like himself.

"Ali? It's me. Denny."

Without saying a word, Ali pushed the screen door open and stood back to allow her husband to come in the house. As he entered, Denny scanned the neat living room. He could tell the furniture was secondhand, but with her creative eye, Ali had a way of making a room special.

Vibrant green houseplants were everywhere. Lining the windowsills. Hanging from the ceiling in tiered macramé planters. Even sitting on top of the bookcase that used to be in her old dorm room.

Everything in the room seemed alive, making the dead expression in his wife's eyes even more apparent.

Ali lowered herself into a bentwood rocker next to the window. She crossed her arms across her chest—hugging herself as if she were cold.

Denny wondered if Ali was going to say anything. Even ask him to sit down. Or would she let him stand there with his hands shoved in the back pockets of his ragged Levi's? One thing was clear. She wasn't going to make things easy.

"Nice place. Are you renting it?" Denny asked, looking around the room.

Ali fixed him with a cold stare. "My parents lent me the money to buy the house after Mrs. Anderson died. Maya and I couldn't live with them forever. And it was obvious you weren't planning to show up any time soon."

"Al, we need to talk."

"You think?" Ali's eyes sparked with anger before she turned and stared out the window.

Denny's mouth suddenly felt stuffed with cotton. "I had this whole speech planned. To try and explain why I had to do what I did."

"You mean why you had to abandon your wife and daughter." Ali's voice began to rise. "The least you can do is say the words. You abandoned your family."

Denny sank down in an old armchair. "Come on, babe—"

Ali glared at her husband. "Don't. Call. Me. That."

Denny put up his hands. "What? Babe? I can't call you babe?"

Ali turned away.

"Will you at least let me explain what happened?" Denny pressed on. "Why I couldn't come—"

Ali didn't let him finish. "I already know the whole sordid story. I heard it from two very impatient men from the federal government. Your buddies from the FBI."

Denny stood up and began pacing a small path on the hardwood floor like a caged animal. "The feds came here to talk to you? You weren't anywhere near Chicago. Why would they—"

"Of course they came to talk to me, Denny. And your parents. And anyone in town who ever passed you on the street when we were growing up. It's been a real gas being the wife of the guy with his picture hanging in the post office. I was lucky anyone in town had the guts to hire me. I don't know what Maya and I would have done if Pat hadn't let me come to work for her in the flower shop."

"Ali, I'm so sorry. I never meant to drag you into this. That's why I didn't come back all these months." He knelt in front of Ali's chair. "I missed you and Maya so much."

Denny saw Ali's eyes shift to the doorway leading from the hall, where he guessed the bedrooms were located. He turned around to see a sleepy, golden-haired toddler rubbing her eyes.

Maya. Tears sprang to his eyes. Could this little person really be his daughter?

Denny pivoted on his haunches and stretched out his arms. "Maya. Baby. You're so grown up," he croaked around the lump in his throat.

The little girl's green eyes grew wide as confusion clouded her face. She looked at Denny. Then over his shoulder to Ali.

"Maya. Sweetie. It's me. Daddy."

At Denny's words, the child's face crumpled and she began to cry. Ali pushed past him and scooped up the little girl.

"It's okay, baby. Mama's here." Ali held the toddler close and patted her on the back.

Maya stuck her thumb in her mouth and buried her face in Ali's shoulder. Ali rubbed her back. "Denny, she hasn't seen you for a while. She'll calm down in a few minutes."

What did he expect? His daughter hadn't seen him for almost nine months. She was only a baby then. Not even walking. She had no idea who he was. He was just some grizzly-bearded man. It made sense she was scared. But it still felt like a knife had been plunged into the center of his heart.

Denny shoved his hands in the pockets of his green army-surplus jacket. "Maybe I better split. And come back later."

"That might be a good idea." Ali looked up. "Let me get Maya calmed down, and then we can talk. Okay?"

"Yeah, sure." Denny turned and walked out the door without looking back. He didn't want Ali to see the tears that had begun to stain his cheeks. She had enough to worry about.

●

Denny sat at the long counter at a truck stop a few miles from Rock Port. He knew he didn't blend in and didn't care. He was tired of hiding.

A chubby waitress in a tight blue uniform set a bowl of steaming chili and a wedge of cornbread in front of him. "Here ya go. Eat it while it's hot."

Denny nodded his thanks. The dish was called Heartburn in a Bowl. He'd ordered it thinking that heartburn was better than the numbness he'd felt since walking out the door of Ali's house while Maya sobbed in her arms.

Denny ate the spicy concoction slowly. By the time he finished the last spoonful, he had made a decision.

"How 'bout some dessert?" The waitress took out her pad. "I've got apple—"

"No thanks," Denny interrupted her calorie-laden sales pitch. "But could I borrow a pen and a sheet of paper?"

"Sure thing, honey." The waitress walked, hips swinging, toward the cash register, where a jelly jar was stuffed with pens. By the time she returned, Denny had most of the letter already composed in his mind.

Dear Ali,

First I want to apologize for involving you in this war against our oppressive, fascist government. I know you have never shared my strong feelings about The Revolution. But after witnessing firsthand the brutality in Chicago, I am convinced that collective, armed defense is needed to protect our community against the threat of an expanding police state. I came to Rock Port to tell you in person that I can't, in good conscience, abandon this Cause.

Although I can't be specific, I want you to know a little bit about the work we are doing to help you understand why I am so committed to The Revolution. Our community is creating collective institutions to make our ideas for just public policy and equitable lifestyle a reality. We are building a Tenants' Union to address housing conditions, a Free Clinic to meet health needs, a Food Co-op to provide nutritional sup-port, and a Peoples' Architecture to deal with environmental issues.

We are moving toward a self-sustaining community through work collectives and communes. I have full confidence that the talent and energies exist within the community to make our dream of a nonex-ploitative society for our brothers and sisters throughout the oppressed world a reality. Although our work is far from complete, it is a new be-ginning. And it is a beginning worth defending.

Again, I hope you can understand my commitment to this Cause. I

*also hope this realization gives you the freedom to build the kind of life
that brings you and Maya peace and satisfaction.*

As Denny signed his name, he hoped the note sounded credible. He had
done his best to make the work sound exciting. Important. He needed to communicate passion and make Ali believe he was committed to The Cause. To the
life he had chosen over them. This would make it easier for Ali to go on with her
own life. And for Maya to forget that he was ever her daddy.

Denny waited until Ali and Maya were likely sleeping. Then he drove into
Rock Port and quietly slipped the note through the mail slot in the front door.

His throat was tight with unshed tears as he climbed into Camille for the
long trip back to California.

To the life he despised and The Cause he now questioned.

It was all he had left.

chapter
TWENTY-FOUR

BEEF STEW

1 1/2 pounds stew meat

2 teaspoons minced garlic

1 tablespoon oil

1 (16 ounce) can diced tomatoes

2 cups beef broth

1 cup red wine

3 carrots, peeled and sliced

1 large onion, peeled and cut into chunks

2 potatoes, peeled and cut into 1-inch chunks

1 tablespoon Worcestershire sauce

1/2 teaspoon thyme

1/2 teaspoon marjoram

1 bay leaf

1/2 cup water

1/4 cup flour

Instructions

1. Cook meat and garlic in oil until meat is brown on all sides (5–7 minutes).

2. Place meat mixture, tomatoes, beef broth, wine, carrots, onion, potatoes, and spices in a slow cooker. Cook on low 8–10 hours or high 5–6 hours.

3. Mix flour and water in small bowl. Slowly whisk into stew. Cook on high 10 minutes until stew is slightly thickened.

Serves 4-6.

OATMEAL BREAD
Uses a bread machine

1/2 cup old-fashioned oats (not quick-cooking)

2 tablespoons butter

1 1/2 teaspoons salt

4 tablespoons honey

1 egg, beaten

3 cups bread flour

2 teaspoons yeast

Instructions

1. Soak oats in one cup boiling water until water is warm—but not hot. Place mixture in bread machine.
2. Add remaining ingredients in the order specified by your bread machine. If you don't know, just add them in the order given.
3. Bake on light setting.

hat was it?" asks Marina. "He never came back?"

Ali shrugs. "Not as far as I know."

Mary Alice looks into her mother's eyes. "I'm so sorry. That had to really hurt."

Ali gently rolls her shoulders. "How about if we put all this ancient history aside and focus on something more pleasant—like dinner? I have some Beef Stew in my slow cooker at home and a loaf of my famous Oatmeal Bread. I was hoping you might be able to join me."

Mary Alice takes her mother's hands in her own. "Mother, we can't keep avoiding this subject. We need to talk. *I* need to talk."

Ali sighs and rubs her eyes with her thumb and index finger. "Sweetheart, it's so hard to put into words. Sure I was hurt. Angry. *Furious* is a better word. But what surprised me was that I wasn't disappointed. I knew your father was idealistic. He was passionate about making the world a better place. And he was one of those people who couldn't close his eyes when he saw an injustice. That's what made me fall in love with him."

"But weren't you bitter that he chose his Cause over you?" asks Mary Alice. "I can't imagine abandoning my family for any reason."

As I listen to M.A. and her mom, I wonder if this is an innate difference between men and women. I agree with Mary Alice. I can't imagine leaving my family to slay some societal dragon.

"Maya, you have to understand that it was a different time back then. There seemed to be no middle ground in the sixties. It was a lot like Dickens wrote in *A Tale of Two Cities*—'It was the best of times, it was the worst of times.'"

"So, how did you do it? How did you manage to raise me alone?"

"Honestly Maya, I don't know. It wasn't easy, and I'd prefer not to have to go through those hard times again. But God had blessed me with a beautiful daughter—and very supportive parents. And, of course, Pat was always flexible with my work schedule here at the shop."

"Who's Pat?" I ask. "I thought you owned Ali's Flowers."

Ali laughed, eyes crinkling at the corners. "Pat used to tease me that I worked like the shop was my own. But that was just because I loved what I was doing. That's probably why she sold it to me for a song when she retired."

"That's not true, Mother," countered Mary Alice. "I saw you putting away money each week in hope of starting your own business someday. Frankly, I don't know how you did it."

Ali smiled at her daughter. "My mom used to tell me that a woman is like a tea bag. You never know how strong she is until she's in hot water."

Ali's comment brings a chuckle from everyone—except Marina.

"So Ali, you're telling us that M.A.'s dad sticks a note in your mail slot—and *poof!*—disappears. And the reason is because he's gonna change the world by bombing banks and blowing up statues."

"This one doesn't mince words, does she?" Ali turns back to Marina. "I can't argue with the facts. But it sounded much more palatable in the sixties, when people in The Movement would say they were 'working to rid the world of injustice.' Maybe I just wanted to believe the best of Denny.'"

"Well, that's what I'm getting at. From what I read in those letters—"

Ali turns to Mary Alice. "I thought you hadn't read the letters yet."

"I haven't but—"

"She hasn't but I have," Marina interrupts. "It's a long story, and Lizzie here has already read me the riot act for invasion of privacy—and who knows what else. But that's beside the point now."

I have to hand it to Marina—she has guts. Just look at her—faster than a sleazy lawyer. Trampling civil liberties in a single bound. The worst

nightmare of the ACLU. Before I have a chance to fully develop this sce-
nario, Marina's words chase all thoughts of constitutional trauma from
my mind.

"What I'm trying to say is that I think the whole Revolution thing
was a ruse." Marina taps the stack of letters with the tip of her fiery red
fingernail. "It doesn't jibe with what he wrote here."

Marina picks up the stack of letters and begins to flip through them.
"Listen to some of what he wrote . . ."

August 30, 1969

*Today you are two years old. It's taking every ounce of self-control
not to be there to help you celebrate. But I am convinced the best gift
I can give you is to stay out of your life. To cushion you from the disillusionment I find myself mired in . . .*

August 30, 1972

*I've learned a lot about the human capacity to adapt to evil. To ac-
cept it and call it by pretty names. To forget what is inconvenient and
to lie about the rest . . .*

August 30, 1975

*Mine is the story of someone permanently disillusioned. It's harder
to live in the world, seeing people as they are. One learns to be silent, in
order to get along. Because the alternative is to find life much too hard
to bear . . .*

August 30, 1980

*There was a time I thought I could change the world. Now all I care
about is getting through the day. A guy once told me a person can sur-
vive either in reality or a dream. It's always his choice . . .*

Marina tosses the stack of letters on the chest. "See what I mean? Those aren't the words of some radical passionate about his Cause. I'm thinkin' he figured out that who he thought were the good guys turned out to be the outlaws. I see that a lot in my line of work."

Ali's face is a portrait of grief. "Although I'd recognize his handwriting anywhere, that sure doesn't sound like the Denny I knew. This was a man completely bogged down by his past. It breaks my heart."

I feel the weight of Denny's disillusionment. I can understand at least a part of it since I've experienced some of the same feelings myself. Disappointed by leaders—even in my own church—who said one thing, then did another. By unscrupulous bosses and coworkers who took advantage of others to advance their own careers. Even by a friend I found out had talked behind my back.

But I've always found a way through the disappointment in myself and others with God's help. *Maybe Denny tried to work through it alone.* I wonder.

"If he was so disillusioned by The Cause, why didn't he just come home? Admit he made a mistake?" Mary Alice asks.

Kelly, who has been uncharacteristically quiet, clears her throat. "Sometimes it's pride. More often it's because the person can't forgive himself. That may have been what happened to Denny."

Mary Alice looks as miserable as Denny's letters sound. "I have so many questions. He wouldn't have written all those letters if he didn't care about me."

Ali reaches out and takes her daughter's hand. "Oh, Maya, of course he cared. He loved you very much. And I know he loved me. I'm beginning to think Denny got caught up in something and couldn't find his way out."

"I wish I could talk to him." Mary Alice's green eyes are lined with red.

Marina clears her throat. "Actually, I might be able to arrange that. That is, if you really want me to."

Now I wonder about Marina's grasp of reality. I mean, the girl has confidence, but this is ridiculous.

Kelly cuts straight to the chase. "Come on, Rina, this is no time to kid around. What are you talking about?"

"I got an e-mail this week regarding the whereabouts of one Dennis Howard O'Brien, born April 1946 in Rock Port, Missouri."

Mary Alice sits forward. "You mean they found his body? Where he's buried?"

Marina raises an eyebrow. "I'm not sure where you got your information about your dad's death, M.A. But he's far from being six feet under."

This is getting ridiculous. "Spit it out, Marina. What are you trying to tell us?" I pick up my glass to take a drink. Marina seems to get a perverse pleasure out of making people sweat.

"Ouch." Marina puts her hand up in front of her as if she's trying to ward off a blow. "I ran a check and found out your dad is serving five years at a Federal Penitentiary Camp in Leavenworth, Kansas."

Now it's my turn to drop a sugary drink on the floor.

chapter
TWENTY-FIVE

"WHEN LIFE GETS STICKY, DIP IT IN CHOCOLATE" COOKIES

1 package semi-sweet chocolate chips

Assorted cookies (Nutter Butter, Oreo, Nilla Wafers, etc.)

Toppings (shredded coconut, chopped nuts, etc.)

Instructions

1. Melt chocolate in a bowl in microwave on medium power, being careful not to burn it. Stir frequently.
2. Dip one half of each cookie into melted chocolate. Then immediately dip in 1 or more toppings.
3. Place on wax paper to allow chocolate to harden.

$\mathcal{H}$ey, Chap!" Marina waves to the tall silver-haired man in a black short-sleeved shirt and clerical collar who is just inside the doorway of the crowded visitors' room at the Federal Penitentiary Camp in Leavenworth, Kansas. This was the same door Mary Alice, Marina, and I had walked through after being processed by a team of bored-looking correction officers.

The process was much easier than I had expected. Especially after Marina's call earlier that morning. . . .

●

$\mathcal{L}$iz, I'm glad I got a hold of you before we left. I want to make sure you're not surprised by the processing procedures at the prison."

"Do I need to bring anything special?" My heart began to beat a little faster.

"Just your ID—and don't wear khaki. That's what the inmates wear. Oh yeah—and be prepared for a strip search."

I gulped. "A strip search? You have to be kidding! Rina, I'm not sure I can—"

"Don't be a wimp, Liz."

As I pressed *Off* on the cordless phone, I was grateful Jess had brought over a batch of our FAC signature treat—"When Life Gets Sticky, Dip It in Chocolate" Cookies—to take along on the three-hour trip to Kansas. It wasn't until I received my visitor's badge and asked directions to the "search area" that I found out the joke was on me. It had taken Marina ten minutes to quit laughing.

I am going to get her for this. I'm not sure how and when. But I will get her good . . .

●

$\mathcal{I}$ am still plotting my revenge as the kind-looking man Marina told us was one of the prison chaplains picks his way through the maze of tables and chairs.

"Marina, it's so good to see you." The chaplain shakes her hand warmly. "And from that bar on your collar it looks like you're playing with the big boys now."

Marina winks. "You can call me Lieut."

The chaplain's warm laugh is like a balm in the chaotic atmosphere of the visitors' room. "These must be your friends," he says, addressing Mary Alice and me.

"Liz Harris." I start to get up from my chair to shake his hand.

"No need to get up, my dear. I'm Pastor Dale." The chaplain shakes my hand, then shifts his attention to Mary Alice. "And you must be Maya."

Marina and I exchange a nervous glance at the mention of M.A.'s childhood name. But we needn't have worried.

Mary Alice smiles and shakes his hand. "Yes, I am, and I can't tell you how much I appreciate your pushing through the paperwork to set up this visit on such short notice. My mother also asked me to thank you for arranging her visit next month."

Pastor Dale sits down, waving away the compliment. "Not a problem. The Duty Officer owed me a favor. Plus it gives me an excuse to catch up with Marina—uh, I mean *Lieutenant* Favazza."

Marina had explained on the trip down that she knew Pastor Dale from the days he used to work with inmates at the Douglas County Jail in downtown Omaha. He was the person she'd turned to for counseling when her husband had left her for another woman. The chaplain had transferred to the federal facility at Leavenworth last year.

"O'Brien family!" The guard's shout draws our attention to the gray metal door at the opposite end of the visitors' room. A man of average height with a bald pate framed by curly white hair stands next to him. Rimless glasses catch glimmers of the fluorescent light as he scans the room. His eyes widen with recognition when Mary Alice turns around in her chair.

Marina takes Mary Alice's hand from across the table. "You gonna be okay, chica?"

Mary Alice draws in a deep breath. "I think so."

I can't fathom the range of emotions churning through Mary Alice. Is she frightened?

Excited?

Confused?

Angry?

Or a jumble of all of the above?

This has to be one of the most difficult times of her life. I also know the best thing—and the only thing—I can do for her is pray. I close my eyes.

Lord, please help my dear friend. She looks grown-up and put-together, but you know the hurt little girl crouching inside. Hold that child close and surround her with the peace that only you can give.

I open my eyes to see the man standing on the other side of the small table. From the moment he lowers himself into the plastic chair, he doesn't take his eyes—now shining with tears—off his daughter.

"Maya, I've hoped for this day for almost as long as I can remember. But I never actually believed it would come. I have so much to tell you, sweetheart . . ."

●

April, 2001

Denny stood at the bottom of the trail leading deep into the towering red-woods. The staff at the Christian camp where he worked told him the trail led to Inspiration Point. He had scoffed when he first heard the name. These days there was little in life that inspired him.

Until he met Joy, that is. Even now, Denny smiled at the memory . . .

●

"My given name is Joyce," said the old woman who described her age as the downhill side of seventy. "But call me Joy. It helps me remember to do what the Bible says and 'count it all joy.'"

At the time, Denny simply nodded and smiled. He'd come across his share of crazy old ladies in his almost thirty years of living in the Santa Cruz area of California. Eccentric didn't even begin to describe some of the people who called this part of the country home.

But the longer he worked with Joy, serving ice cream and pop at the little shop the camp had dubbed the Soda Fountain, the more he began to realize that her joy came from something deep inside. And her sweetness bubbled out like one of the clear mountain streams that flowed through the property.

Denny's job at the camp basically consisted of hauling ice and washing dishes. The work was physical—but not too demanding. Almost sixty years old, Denny was grateful for a break from the road crew or landscaping jobs he had survived on since cutting ties with Rob and the others in the underground. On slow afternoons, he and Joy passed the time by playing Scrabble behind the counter.

"Gotta take a load off these feet," she said, setting the game board up on a round table. "You a good speller?"

Denny grinned. "I won a spelling bee in junior high."

"Then I guess you'll do."

For the first time in many years, Denny began to look forward to his job—and the afternoon Scrabble game with Joy. As their friendship grew, Denny mustered up the nerve to broach what he'd begun to think of as the "joy thing."

"How do you do it?" Denny asked, lining up the lettered tiles on the board to form the word *sandwich*. "I mean, there's so much sadness and disappointment in life. How can you be so happy all the time? You haven't had an easy life."

Joy didn't answer Denny's question right away. After a few minutes, she looked up from the word she was working on and fixed her gaze on him. "I've lived a long time and have come to realize that the answer to your question is something everybody's gotta figure out for themselves."

"But—"

Joy held up a crooked finger to silence him. "I'll tell you what. I got a friend down in Santa Cruz. Her name's Linda, and she owns a bookstore out on Souquel."

"I think I know it," Denny said. "The Garden or—"

"No, this is strictly a Christian store. It's called Linda's Bible Bookstore. Get yourself a good Bible. Linda will help you find a good translation."

"I don't want to offend you, Joy, but Christianity's not my bag. I grew up in the Midwest and had my fill of—"

"Have you read the Bible?"

"Not the whole thing, but I'm familiar with the teachings of Jesus and—"

"Start with the New Testament in the book of John." Joy drew a tile from the box and cocked her head toward Denny. "He was the sensitive disciple. Just like you, son."

Denny hadn't realized how much he had missed hearing someone call him "son." Or the hole that simple word could fill.

●

It had been six months since Joy suggested Denny visit her friend Linda's bookstore. Since that time, he'd read the entire New Testament. Three times.

As Denny began the slow trek up to Inspiration Point this afternoon, he still wasn't sure what he'd find. Or exactly why he was going. All he knew was that something had to change. It was getting too hard to roll out of bed each morning and face the wasteland that had become his life.

As Denny hiked along the redwood trail, he ticked off the people he had admired as a young man.

Abbie Hoffman—found dead of a drug overdose in 1989.

Norman Mailer—married six times.

Jerry Rubin—Yippie turned Yuppie, complete with a cushy job on Wall Street.

Timothy Leary—videotaped for a documentary in the final delirium of death repeating the phrase "Why not?" over and over.

And the minstrels of the music that had inspired an entire generation. Janis Joplin. Jim Morrison. Jerry Garcia. Dead from a life of excess. Or despair. Or both.

Denny felt the weight of these images as he walked through the silent forest. Linked with the futility of his own life, they forged a heavy chain that was too much for him to carry. He longed to give in. To allow the chain to pull him into the abyss with other disillusioned souls.

Come to me all who labor and are heavy laden, and I will give you rest.

The words of Jesus recorded in the book of Matthew haunted him. Called him. Prodded him to move on.

Come to me . . .

Could he trust those words? Could he trust the One who said them? Or were they like the empty promises of his youth?

By the time Denny reached the summit, he was so spent that all he could do was fall on his face. At the foot of the cross.

"I'm sorry," he moaned, spittle mixing with the dirt. "I'm so sorry."

Come to me . . .

"But it's my fault. All mine. I don't deserve forgiveness."

Come to me . . .

"I'm not worthy."

Because of my Son, you are my son.

●

The sounds of the chaotic visitors' room—babies crying, children running, chairs scraping, doors clanging—fade to nothing as I listen to Denny O'Brien speak. His story is so powerful, so real, that I feel I am with him at the foot of the cross on Inspiration Point.

Denny wipes a tear from his eye with the back of his hand. "I don't remember how long I lay there on my face in the shadow of the cross. But when I got up, I felt lighter. Different. I still don't completely understand what happened up there, but I knew I was different when I came down. I belonged."

*ch*APTER TWENTY-SIX

OLD-FASHIONED ICE-CREAM SODAS

Although there are lots of variations, an ice-cream soda is basically a flavoring, seltzer (or club soda), and ice cream. Whipped cream on top is optional—but delicious. Here's how you make one.

1. Put 2 tablespoons of syrup or flavoring in the bottom of a large glass.
2. Stir in seltzer water or club soda to within 2 inches of the top of the glass.
3. Add 1 large scoop of very hard ice cream.
4. Top the drink off with more seltzer or club soda to get a foamy head.

Ice-cream soda combinations:

Black & White: chocolate syrup, seltzer, and vanilla ice cream

Canary Island Special: vanilla syrup, seltzer, and chocolate ice cream

Black Cow: root beer with vanilla ice cream

Brown Cow: chocolate syrup, cola, and vanilla ice cream

In the Hay: strawberry syrup, seltzer, and vanilla ice cream

Hoboken: pineapple syrup, seltzer, and chocolate ice cream

Boston Cooler: ginger ale and vanilla ice cream

$\mathcal{S}$ome things never change.

It has been a little more than a month since the FAC at my house that put Mary Alice's well-ordered life in a blender—and turned it on high speed. Since that day we have learned that this seemingly average suburban mom can not only organize a closet in record time, but she:

- has lived under an assumed name since 1985;
- owns a 1963 VW minibus and a purple lava lamp;
- is the child of flower children and once lived on a commune;
- will participate in any craft except macramé and tie-dye; and
- is on the approved visitor list for a Federal Penitentiary Camp.

Even with all the upheaval in her life, Mary Alice still kept her turn for FAC. Not only that, she set up her kitchen counter with a darling little soda fountain.

As I said, some things never change.

I used to think this penchant for all things domestic was an attempt to appear perfect to the world. But after seeing her mom's cozy nest, I think this is just Mary Alice's nature. And her gift.

Mary Alice puts a little squirt of whipped cream on Jess's Canary Island Special. "I decided to do the soda fountain in honor of my dad's friend from the Christian camp. The one who wants people to call her Joy."

I loved hearing that story and feel honored that Mary Alice asked me along for the first meeting with her dad. "Maybe there's something to the mixture of ice cream and seltzer water that will bring out more joy in my personality. Hannah says I've been a real grump lately."

Mary Alice hands Marina a Black Cow and sits at the kitchen table with the rest of us. "I'm hoping it will help me be a little more forgiving."

Lucy pats Mary Alice's hand. "It's a process, sweetie. You have to work through the pain."

"On one hand, I'm happy my dad realized he needed to pay for his crime and turned himself in. And, of course, I'm thrilled about his faith."

"It was an amazing story." I take a bite of ice cream.

"I hear a *but* in there," says Kelly.

"But . . . I'm still having trouble letting go of my anger."

Jess passes a box of tissues across the table toward Mary Alice. "That's understandable. Like Lucy said, It's going to take time."

"That's what my mom told me. But she doesn't seem to be nearly as bitter as I am. In fact, she said her visit with my dad went very well." Mary Alice snatches a tissue from the box and blows her nose. "I suffered all these years not having a dad. It was embarrassing. I was lonely. And I never felt like I was good enough for someone to love. Why do children always end up paying for the poor choices their parents make?"

Ouch! I start to think about some of the dumb choices I've made lately. The most recent being caving to pressure to serve on a school committee that causes me to miss Hannah's volleyball games on Tuesday nights. Maybe that's the real reason we're not getting along lately.

"Remember, M.A., your dad is paying for the choices he made," says Kelly. "He paid in the pain of not knowing his daughter. The guilt he carried all those years. Through giving up his marriage. And now he's in prison."

Mary Alice drums her fingers on the table. "Sure he's paying his debt to society. But what about me? And my mother? He owes us, too."

Marina stands up and squirts more chocolate in her Black Cow. "I've got another stupid criminal story. Wanna hear it?"

Marina's stupid criminal stories are hilarious. One of my favorites has to do with a guy who robbed a convenience store but left a wallet containing his driver's license on the counter.

"There's this guy who was in debt up to his eyeballs," Marina says, lounging against the counter. "He owed his boss somethin' like a half-million bucks. He'd postdated a check or somethin' and wasn't good for it."

Kelly gasps. "Who would write a check for that kind of money when he didn't have it? Like a half-million dollars is just going to show up in your bank account."

I laugh. "Maybe he was waiting for one of those deposits from Nigeria. Where some deposed king needs a place to deposit his money so the militia doesn't steal it."

"Lizzie, didn't you call me about one of those scams last year, asking if it was legit?" Marina raises a perfectly shaped eyebrow at me as she plops down at the table across from Mary Alice.

The red spots start to bloom on my neck. "Maybe . . ."

"Anyway, the boss asks him about it—and he spills his guts," says Marina. "The guy tells his boss he doesn't have the money. Doesn't know what to do. Yada Yada."

Sounds like one of my kids trying to get an advance on allowance.

"The boss has the right to have him picked up for passing a bad check." Marina pauses and takes a sip of her ice-cream soda. "But he doesn't."

Kelly scowls. "He let the guy get away with it? A half-million bucks?"

"That's right. The boss says to just forget about it. Even says the guy doesn't have to pay him back. Ever."

Jess laughs. "I hope he got it in writing."

"But listen—it gets more interesting." Marina swirls the straw in her ice-cream soda. "The guy gets home and opens up his mail to find a letter from his bank telling him the fifty-dollar check he had deposited from a buddy bounced. It seems his buddy wasn't good for the fifty bucks he owed him."

"That was good timing for the friend," says Mary Alice. "Did he call the guy up and tell him to forget about the debt?"

Marina smiles. "You'd think. Instead he decides to have the sheriff haul the guy in for passing the bad check."

"For fifty dollars? After his boss forgave him five hundred thousand?" I ask "That's so wrong."

"Well . . . the guy was within his rights. His buddy broke the law." Marina pulls her shoulders back and stretches. "But the story doesn't end there. The boss hears about the arrest. Puts two and two together and—*bing-bang-boom*—has the jerk tossed in jail too. Except now the jerk is facing ten to twenty in the federal pen."

Kelly shakes her head. "That's not just stupid, it's sad. Where'd you read about it?"

"It came from a trusted source." Marina winks. "The Bible."

Lucy smiles. "The parable of the unforgiving servant."

"That's the one," says Marina. "See Luce, I've been keeping up with my Bible study."

"Good girl."

Marina looks out the window. "That story helped me get over the bitterness I had for my ex-husband. I was so mad at what Bobby did to me and the girls. He deserved pain. Lots of it."

No argument from any of us. We'd all had a front-row seat for the torture Bobby put Marina through.

"But when I read about Jesus telling this story to his disciples, I realized that not forgiving Bobby wasn't just hurting him. It put me in prison too." Marina takes a spoonful of the ice cream while her words sink in. "And although this was harder to take, I was forced to admit that I wasn't perfect either. I know you guys think I have it all together. But trust me, I have my moments."

What I wouldn't give for one drop of Marina's confidence.

Or her metabolism, as I watch her get up to make another ice-cream soda.

"So I figured what's good for the goose is good for the gander. If God can forgive me, the least I can do is forgive Bobby." She frowns. "It doesn't mean I don't want to clean his clock every once in a while. Especially when he hurts one of the girls' feelings. But when I start feeling that way, I try to think of that good-for-nothin' servant who tossed his buddy in jail for fifty bucks. Works for me."

It's annoying when Marina's right. Not because she's right, but because she makes no attempt to soften the blow.

How many grudges am I holding on to? I still get mad every time I think of my brother drawing a mustache on my Mrs. Beasley doll with permanent marker on Christmas Day, 1970. I bring it up every time one of the girls opens a Christmas gift that happens to be a doll. Of course I say I'm just teasing. And everyone laughs at the funny way I tell the story. But I still see the tightness in my brother's face every time I launch into the tale. After more than thirty years, it's probably time to let go.

Unfortunately, Mary Alice has a lot more to forgive than a talking doll with a mustache. She missed out on a relationship with her dad. For what? A stupid mistake in the Sixties. That's a lot to swallow. And from the tears flowing down my friend's face, I know I can't be too far off.

"You're right, Marina. It hurts to hold on to the pain. It's comfortable—but it still hurts."

"It's like when I don't work out," says Kelly. "It may be more comfortable to stay in bed. But if I do, I pay for it later. Even so, I still have to force myself to tie on my running shoes each morning."

Note to self: suggest adding exercise to the list of banned topics for FAC.

"Sweetie, you have to remember that it's a process," says Jess. "And it will be harder if you try and handle it alone."

"Maybe you could talk to your pastor," suggests Lucy.

I grin. "Excellent idea. And while you're at it, could you have him explain to my pastor why we were hauled into jail?"

Marina leans back in her chair and laughs. "That was rich, Lizzie. You shoulda saw your face."

Good thing we are on the subject of forgiveness. I am ready to—how did Rina phrase it?—clean *her* clock.

"I also thought it might help to put together a scrapbook of my dad's photos and mementos. Maybe with Mom."

I hold up my hand like a traffic cop. "Stop! FAC rule violation—no mention of scrapbooking allowed."

Marina grins. "Don't be such a drag, Lizzie."

"Loosen up, Liz. Let go of those puritanical hang-ups," adds Kelly.

Even Jess couldn't resist joining in. "Bad vibes . . ."

As I said, some things never change. On the bright side, it has the makings of a great column.

●

Scrapbooking: A Second Look for the Skeptic
By Elizabeth Harris

Even a 1,000 mile journey starts with a single step.
—Lao-Tzu

In the past, I've made some disparaging comments about the hobby of scrapbooking. A recent experience, however, has prompted me to take a second look at what I once considered an obsessive hobby.

Webster's Dictionary defines a memorial as "something that keeps a memory alive." So, today I ask you, dear reader, how are you keeping your important memories alive? Do you, like me, struggle with what to keep and what to throw out?

Recently, I had one of those proverbial light-bulb moments and came to the conclusion that the real question isn't so much what to keep, but what to leave behind.

What do you want others to remember about you?

About your family?

What will be your legacy to future generations?

This mind-set makes it much easier to muster the courage to toss the corsage from senior prom. And instead preserve those things that provide a genuine account of your journey.

Of course, a scrapbook is one way to chronicle these memories. But I want to encourage you not to stop with cute photos and kitschy souvenirs. Take time to record the feelings, blessings, and lessons connected to these events.

Perhaps you may want to leave behind a well-loved book. If so, take the time to include a note about why the volume is important to you.

And finally, for those of us who like to write, exploit this passion. Keep a journal of prayers or thoughts. Write letters to family members, including more than the current weather conditions and family ailments.

Whatever method you choose to communicate your journey, don't be afraid to show your warts. Your humanness. Otherwise, you might as well leave behind a Barbie doll. Perfect, but also cold, plastic, and lifeless.

Give future generations a peek into the heart of a real person. Who just happens to have a great scrapbook.

Loving life!

Liz

As I press *Send* to once again ship my column through cyberspace, I wonder what my children will remember about me. Will they think about our fun times together—or the time spent nagging about chores? Will they picture me on a good-hair day—or with bed head? Lofty thoughts for a Saturday morning.

As Scarlett O'Hara said, "I'll think about that tomorrow." But in the meantime, I am going to dust off that half-finished scrapbook. And remove any and all pictures with bed head.

DISCUSSION QUESTIONS

1. **The primary characters in the book are the six female members of the Friday Afternoon Club.**
   - What attracts you, as a woman, to a group or a club?
   - What are the differences between clubs with all female members, as opposed to those with female and male members? How do you respond differently?

2. **The women of the Friday Afternoon Club get together each week for no purpose other than because they enjoy each other's company.**
   - What benefits have they reaped from investing in friendship? What needs are met?
   - What does it mean practically to invest in friendship? Share a story of when friendship meant a lot to you. Or of when someone told you your friendship meant a lot to her.
   - What things stand in the way of investing in friendship with other women? How have you overcome these obstacles?

3. **The characters in the Friday Afternoon Club have very different personalities.**
   - Who do you most relate to? Why?
   - Who do you least relate to? Why?

- Who is your favorite character? Why?
- Who is your least favorite character? Why?

4. The main character, Liz Harris, is a lifestyle columnist for the local newspaper and struggles with both her public persona as a "domestic diva" and the reality that her home is less than perfect.
   - Do you think this is a common issue with women? Why or why not?
   - What are the risks and benefits of allowing others to see us as we really are? (If you have a good story regarding this, why not share it?)

5. The Friday Afternoon Club is proactive in helping Mary Alice deal with her feelings of abandonment by her father.
   - How would you feel if your friends "ambushed" you in such a way?
   - Why are we often hesitant to take a proactive approach with friends?
   - What could you do to help a friend through a difficult time?

6. One of the themes of the book is the impact of personal choices on the lives of others. Consider the following characters. What effect did their choices have on themselves and others?
   - Denny
   - Mary Alice
   - Ali

- Liz
- Marina
- What choices have you made that have had a positive effect on you and/or your family? Are there any you regret? If so, what are they? And why do you regret them?

7. Another theme in the book deals with forgiveness. In particular, Denny struggles with forgiving himself, and Mary Alice struggles with forgiving her father.
   - Why do you think forgiveness is such a difficult issue for most people? What kinds of things stand in the way of forgiving another person? How about accepting forgiveness?
   - Near the end of the book, Marina paraphrased a parable from the Bible (Matthew 18:21–35), commonly referred to as the parable of the unforgiving servant. What was her point? How might this apply to a situation you may be struggling with?

8. The Friday Afternoon Club has a list of "banned topics" that aren't supposed to be brought up when the friends are together. It includes "scrapbooking."
   - Why do you think scrapbooking is included on the list?
   - Do you scrapbook? Why or why not?
   - At the end of the book, Liz takes a fresh look at scrapbooking. Why does Liz change her mind about this hobby? Do Liz's words change or confirm your mind about this topic in any way?

- How could you preserve and communicate the values and memories that are important to you—whether in a scrapbook or any other form? Share some practical ideas . . . and then carve out a few minutes to start on an idea this week!

ABOUt THE AUtHOR

$\mathcal{C}$yndy Salzmann is a wife and mother who does much of her writing on the back of fast-food wrappers—usually while waiting to pick up her kids. Desperate for an excuse to avoid laundry, Cyndy decided to write three Christian nonfiction books on home management for the "domestically challenged," launch a national speaking career, work as a Christian radio personality, and teach her children how to sort colors. *Crime & Clutter* is her second novel and Book Two in the Friday Afternoon Club mystery series. Book One, *Dying to Decorate,* was released in 2005.

Cyndy has been married for twenty-five years to John Salzmann, her college sweetheart and the most patient man in the world. They are blessed with three children: Freddy (21), Liz (19), and Anna (14). And, yes, the family also has a precocious Westie named Daisy, who loves to scavenge in the trash.

In her spare time, Cyndy loves to cook, read, and work on family scrapbooks. This last pursuit allows her to permanently destroy any photos of herself she doesn't consider flattering.

Finally, but most importantly, Cyndy loves God with all her heart and has committed her life to following His lead, even if it means airing all her dirty laundry. Literally.

Other books by Cyndy Salzmann

Dying to Decorate: A Friday Afternoon Club Mystery

Making Your Home a Haven: Strategies for the Domestically Challenged

The Occasional Cook: Culinary Strategies for Overcommitted Families

Want to Contact Cyndy?

You may write her via e-mail at cyndy@familyhavenministries.com, or through her website: www.cyndysalzmann.com.

A free subscription to her newsletter is available by sending a blank e-mail to subscribe@familyhavenministries.com.

rECIPE indEX

ANOTHER FRIDAY AFTERNOON CLUB MYSTERY

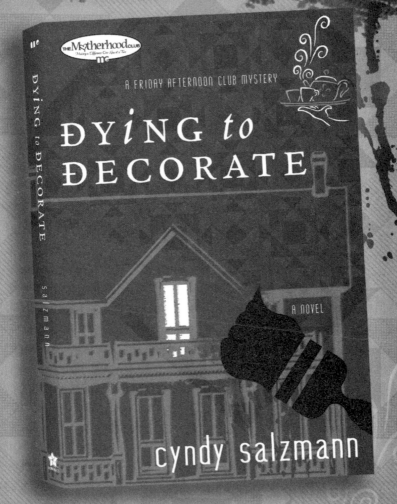

A feisty group of six moms—dubbed the Friday Afternoon Club—find themselves acting as sleuths to unravel the mysteries they encounter when one of them inherits a Civil War-era mansion. Includes a variety of recipes that tie into the story!

HOWARD BOOKS
A DIVISION OF SIMON & SCHUSTER

ISBN: 1-58229-455-0 • $12.99
Available wherever books are sold.